Discussing Wittgenstein

ANN DRYSDALE

Published by Cinnamon Press
Meirion House
Glan yr afon
Tanygrisiau
Blaenau Ffestiniog
Gwynedd LL41 3SU
www.cinnamonpress.com

The right of Ann Drysdale to be identified as author of this work
has been asserted by her in accordance with the Copyright,
Designs and Patent Act, 1988. © 2009 Ann Drysdale
ISBN 978-1-905614-68-4
British Library Cataloguing in Publication Data. A CIP record for
this book can be obtained from the British Library

Designed and typeset in Palatino by Cinnamon Press
Cover image: Bud Handelsman © *Punch* Ltd
Cover design by Mike Fortune-Wood
Printed in Great Britain by the MPG Books Group,
Bodmin and King's Lynn

The publisher acknowledges the financial support of the Welsh
Books Council

Acknowledgements

The Bud Handelsman cartoon on the cover is reproduced with the permission of *Punch* Ltd.

The quotation from William Empson's *This Last Pain* is used with the permission of Penguin Group (UK).

Thanks also to Peterloo Poets for permission to quote from the Collected Poems of UA Fanthorpe and to Harry Chambers in particular for allowing the author to reproduce personal correspondence.

Never stay up on the barren heights of cleverness but come down into the green valleys of silliness…
If people did not sometimes do silly things, nothing intelligent would ever get done…

Translated phrases opportunistically cherry-picked from the work of Ludwig Wittgenstein

"What is conceivable can happen too"
Said Wittgenstein, who had not dreamt of you;
But wisely, if we worked it long
We should forget where it was wrong.

From 'This Last Pain'
William Empson

Foreword

Can anyone writing today match Ann Drysdale's blend of poetry and prose? I have yet to find them. In *Three-three, two-two, five-six* she told a heart-rending story. Her partner, Philip (Hospital Number 332256) was treated for bowel cancer, with subsequent miserable (and often humiliating) complications. In the middle of all this, there was a marriage, a number of poems, some tears and laughter. At the end of the volume, Philip (who narrowly survived the hospital experience) was transported home with a walking stick called 'High Risk' and very mixed feelings about his discharge.

Discussing Wittgenstein continues the story. For anyone who read the previous volume and ended, like me, thinking *'But what happened next?'* it is a must. It is primarily a love story, of course. And like any great love story, it is both ordinary and unique. Ann and Philip, the wedded lovers, are united by laughter, divided by illness. It is not easy writing about the last months of a person you love. Drysdale does it unsentimentally (this is a book that will make you laugh) and with perfect pacing. A section of prose narrative is followed by a poem: that is the simple structure. Often the poem tells a little story too, or fits into the big narrative. It is pragmatic ("Spirituality is not my thing"), lyrical ("the loneliness and hopelessness of Lydney in the rain") and it brings death, which we so neatly sidestep these days, squarely into the living room: "And no part of the man I loved was distasteful to me, even the wretched effluents of his death". It is hard to say how and why an account of a man's deterioration and demise should be *pleasurable* to read—but it is a joy to encounter such clean, truthful, balanced, beautiful writing. And it is not about death at all really: it is about life.

Helena Nelson

Discussing Wittgenstein

Coming Home

When Philip was discharged from hospital he had been there for almost three months, but he returned home from a much farther place than Abergavenny. At one stage it had been touch and go whether he would come home at all. As it was, he brought back with him an indwelling catheter, a ramshackle colostomy, a perineal fistula and a wide-open abdominal wound.

We came back to the big house at number 20, the house Philip loved and could no longer afford to keep. It was already on the market but I had asked the agents not to put up a 'For Sale' sign outside. I took my new responsibilities seriously.

We had first faced the situation as companions but were now man and wife and had to negotiate the significance of this in a new setting. We sat side by side as I justified my obvious executive decisions. This was still Philip's home, but I had had to make changes to it. I had re-appointed the sitting room downstairs with a bed for him and a long plastic runner making a washable path across the carpet to the tiled kitchen. I would sleep beside him on the floor as I had done on the ward. Here we would live for the first few days until he was able to manage the stairs and reclaim the rest of his territory, including the double bedroom we had shared until he was admitted. I wittered to a halt and took a deep breath. He listened and said 'well done', but he looked unsafe and afraid.

The only person he had regularly asked after while he was away was Mavis, whom I had foisted on him as a kitten, after rescuing her from among an illegitimate litter. He always referred to her as 'my little ginger cat' although she is tortoiseshell. He did it to annoy me. This was my own fault. I had corrected him once too often and started to air my knowledge of feline chromosomes until his eyes glazed over and I saw him make up his mind; if she was to be his cat, she would be whatever colour he chose to call her, so there. And after all, it made no difference to Mavis, who soon appeared from nowhere and settled on his lap. I came in with two cups of tea and smiled. "Ah, there's your little ginger cat," I said. "She's missed you." Philip gave me a broad grin and I winked at him.

Care in the Community

Within a day of Philip's discharge from hospital, we met our first District Nurse. Her name was Chris and she knew who we were and what had happened to us. She brought accurate notes with her and fleshed them out with our answers to her cheerful, intelligent questions. Finally, she declared "Ann's doing wonders with the pine end and the plumbing, so no problems there, but we're on call if you need us and we'll supply and apply the dressings for the big one." She told us that we would be visited every other day for as long as necessary, and as far as possible at a time of our choosing. "What time would suit?" she asked, pen poised and glasses gleaming.

She was especially interested in the large open wound on Philip's belly because she was working on a paper on the healing process. Her enthusiasm was heartening. She looked at the red wet ruin of it with a mixture of fascination and respect and asked if she might measure it and make a tracing. Philip nodded and grinned—"so long as you don't press too hard."

One of the things Chris brought with her was a pack of heavy-duty yellow plastic bags. Within the health service, yellow is the colour of contagion. We were to put into these all clinical waste produced by Philip's daily care. They would be collected once a week by a specialist contractor and destroyed, along with the MRSA that had come home from hospital with us and was now our responsibility.

Other members of the team came and went. There was one whose working vocabulary appeared to contain only one verb—'to pop'. She would pop in to pop on a dressing and then pop into the kitchen to pop her hands under the tap and pop on a bit of hand-gel.

At first this irritated me beyond belief but Philip pointed out that she was a nurse, not a novelist, and I was being unrealistic in my expectations. What he meant was that I was a pedantic bitch and, alas, he was right. I made a great effort to forgive and understand. In doing so I realised that this woman was more than a skilled nurse, she was also a trusted confidante flitting between stricken households in a community that was greedy for gossip. Every visit had to be a clean slate, a fresh start. It was better to hand out sticky pop-corn than to risk betraying precious secrets and I grew to respect her for it. I learned to equate a high pop-count with a high stress level and on such occasions I would pop the kettle on and we would dunk a quick biscuit together.

Another regularly came in and shouted so loudly that Philip would wince and recoil. In the end I was forced to ask her to talk a little more quietly. She was utterly silent for a moment and then said, "Thank you." She told me she had got so used to her older patients being either deaf or demented that when she saw grey hair she no longer thought twice before embarking on a great "Hallo-o" as she entered the house, followed by a bellowed interrogation. The assumption, she said, was shameful; it should have occurred to her to ask. She went back into the room where Philip was sitting and apologised cheerfully for her thoughtlessness, thanking me again for calling her attention to it. This example of simple grace left a glow in the room after she had gone.

They were all angels in their different ways. Nevertheless we felt guiltily good when we had learned to cope without them and their visits diminished and stopped. Only Chris continued to call in from time to time. She it was who somehow orchestrated each big breakthrough and was there to celebrate them with us, one by one. The final disappearance of the superbug, the eventual healing of the wound, the removal of the catheter and subsequent re-education of the muscles of micturition, all these we shared with her. The last thing she did for us before she moved on was all the soul-destroying paperwork involved in getting Philip the wheelchair he had never dreamed he would need. We missed her.

Peggotty's House

Philip read Dickens, too, of course he did. However, he was a *Pickwick Papers* man with a passing interest in *A Tale of Two Cities*, whereas I especially loved *David Copperfield*, chiefly because of the characters. Oh, Doady himself I could take or leave and Dora was an oversimplification of my own notional nemesis but I already knew Clara Peggotty and Betsey Trotwood because they were my own grandmothers and Agnes Wickfield became a role model, a benchmark of female excellence to which I aspired. And still do, up to a point.

When Philip bought Number 21, we had no idea that within a year he would be forced to move into it permanently and to sell Number 20, the big house he had lovingly restored as his final home. It was an odd little excrescence, tacked on to the side of Number 20 like a lean-to lavatory. It belonged to an entrepreneur from Exeter who rented it out to ill-assorted individuals, most in receipt of state benefits, so that his profit could be skimmed off at source. They weren't bad people but they made noises of a different kind from ours and lived in a different segment of the day. Things came to a head when a lad called Andrew, setting up a haphazard home there with his monosyllabic baby-mother, lit a bonfire in the front yard that cracked the party wall and scorched one of Philip's beloved roses. I tackled him about it and his reply, *Fuck off—it'll grow again, m'n*, decided the issue. Philip extended the mortgage on Number 20 and put in an offer for Number 21. When Andrew left, his mewling infant having qualified them all for a council house in Winchestown, Philip took possession.

He justified it to the bank as an investment, to himself as a long-term hobby and to me as somewhere for visitors to stay. Which was odd, since neither of us felt at ease with visitors.

At that stage we were still having difficulty coming to terms with each other.

Inside, Number 21 was a disaster. Crumbling floors, damp walls, a non-functioning bathroom and the most spectacular growth of dry rot I had ever seen. This was not so much an insentient fungus as a soft, golden, rapacious animal. I was fascinated by its seminal smell.

Philip would spend hours sitting by himself in there, doing creative visualisation and measuring things. He would come back and tell me excitedly what he intended to do; the traditional kitchen, the walk-in larder, the provision of a bath and the abolition of the existing shower, which was potentially provided by the overflow pipe from the upstairs cistern in Number 20. This actually protruded through the wall above the cracked and lidless lavatory pan in Number 21. A triumph of vernacular architecture—but it would have to go.

Even in hospital, when he had resigned himself to selling Number 20, he drew plans and showed me how it was all going to be. What he had not considered, let alone resigned himself to, was the fact that he would at first be too disabled to undertake the work himself and that, in the absence of funds, I would have to be his eyes and hands until he was better.

In the first few weeks after his discharge, I would get him up and ready to face the day, then go next door and potter, just as he had done, the difference being that I hadn't a fraction of his skill. All I had were his drawings and his dreams. But by this time Number 20 was already on the market and there was no time to waste.

Upstairs in the bedroom, he had started to create a curved ceiling with tongue-and-groove panelling. Seeking a point of reference for me, he had told me it was going to be like Peggotty's house in Yarmouth, which was adapted from an upturned boat. Here he would retreat to live a simple, Shaker life, surrounded by wood and books, pursuing his inner creativity.

He hadn't got very far with it. The room was a sad paradox, contriving to be both dusty and damp. A hopeful stepladder stood by the far wall, rising above the silky filth that only the demolition of ancient ceilings can engender. Above my head the dirty beams still bristled with the flat-headed nails that had held the crumbling laths. What a mess.

One of Philip's elliptical carpenters' pencils, specially designed so as not to roll out of reach, lay on the sloping windowsill doing what it did best. The middle bit of the ceiling—the kelson, so to speak—was in place, but the floor was littered with an alarming amount of offcuts, making it clear that he had not found it easy

Philip had been buying the timber a little at a time from B&Q. There were several tall shrink-wrapped packs leaning like dispirited dossers against the rough-rendered wall. I brought one of them over to the window, picked up the pencil and poked its chiselled point through the plastic. I felt instantly guilty. Philip abhorred any misuse of tools. He would always wait till he had, or could make, the correct instrument for every purpose, while I would see the immediate possibilities in whatever was to hand and use it, like an opportunistic ape.

I pulled out one of the pieces of timber, dragged the stepladder into the middle of the room, climbed unsteadily and eased the fragile tongue gingerly into the waiting groove. I slid the whole thing back to abut with a faint click against the last one Philip had pinned in place, months previously. I had made a start.

For a moment I looked askance at the place where the ceiling would eventually meet the wall and wondered how I would marry the haphazard angle with the predetermined curve. But wotthehell!—by the time I got that far I would know a lot more than I did now. Philip often quoted Goethe on the magical power of simply beginning. A slow happiness took hold. I was almost confident and, in the absence of the master, in control.

Here I was, arms aching and eyes full of sawdust, creating a borrowed dream from inside and underneath, but it was no longer a boat I was building. It was a special vessel to keep the two of us safe from the catastrophe to come. Not a bright ketch to bob merrily on the bosom of the ocean, but a turtle-turned, ready-wrecked, upside-down ark that would hold the last pair of our particular species high and dry on Mount Ararat while the rest of the world went whistling about its business.

The Bright Young Things

That was what Philip called them, the young couple who bought Number 20. A phrase that has lived in the language since the thirties, sidelined now, but still giving off whiffs of criticism, envy and regret.

They both worked at the hospital, he in I.T., she in the purchasing department. They had lived in the area for some time and knew the big house on the small street and had fantasised about living in it one day. Or so they said. He was forging a promising political career in Plaid Cymru and Philip said that the house was probably in keeping with his aspirations. *Just as it once was with yours* said my heart, before I shushed it.

Once the deal was clinched, they were naturally anxious to move in. They rang frequently and the calls always began with "when...?" I did my best to move what I could of what we needed to keep, although Number 21 was still hardly habitable and the more we stuffed into it, the less likely it was ever to become so.

Philip was still too frail to do any of the major shifting and he used what little strength he had to prepare spaces and surfaces for the items I carted round from next door. Before going into hospital he had installed an impressive fitted office in Number 20, convinced it would pay for itself in a few years. Knowing how he would miss it, I was helping him to improvise a study in the other upstairs room in Number 21. Understanding that he would not feel secure until he had it set up to his liking, I encouraged him to plan the workspace and adjust the shelving so that the computer and all its peripherals, photocopier and fax machine, books and hi-fi could be moved in a piece at a time. Where they had been would show me where they would go. It would probably be achievable in a day.

Another phonecall. This time I said yes—they could start moving in at the weekend so long as I could leave the emptying of Philip's study until Monday, when I would move it all while they were at work. They agreed. I told Philip about the arrangement and he was delighted. "Well done," he said.

On Monday we had breakfast, listening for the slamming of their car's doors. We exchanged a thumbs-up. Philip went upstairs to direct operations and I went next door, let myself in and went up to his beloved office.

I think I screamed. The fitted desks and shelves were entirely filled with the files and equipment of the Bright Young Things. At first I could see none of Philip's possessions and then I saw that they had been stacked in a teetering heap by the door.

I had no doubt that it would all be there, somewhere, but the plan I had conceived—the sequential unplugging and steady ferrying of recognisable equipment was now completely out of the question. It all lay in a lump, with wires entangled like the root system of a huge and horribly deformed shrub.

If it had indeed been a shrub I could have stuck two forks in, back to back, and prised it apart, but it wasn't—it was Philip's whole working life and I had no idea where to start. I simply sat and cried until I heard Philip's faltering footsteps in the hall. "Is there a problem?" I told him what had happened.

We managed to move some of it but when the Bright Young Things came back, there was still more remaining than shifted. I explained that I had expected it all to be left as it was and the he-half of the couple, whom Philip had named Young Rush-about, looked aggrieved and claimed he'd done as I asked—"We left it all in the room, like you said. And we got it ready for you, to save time."

There was no answer to that, but I tried anyway. "It's a lot harder to move now it's all piled in a heap." He didn't share my understanding of the importance of order to the man I loved, or even a respect for his treasured equipment; he simply assumed that the poor old woman was having trouble lifting the gear off the floor. He scooped it up in a series of exaggerated armfuls and took each one at a gallop down his stairs and up ours to leave it in an even more confused agglomeration on the desk that Philip had painstakingly cleared.

I could scarcely breathe for the desire to murder the insensitive young Visigoth, but Philip thanked him, shook his hand and asked him to accept "something for his trouble". Then he offered him a cup of tea, which I made and served with what little grace I could muster.

Later we stood together in the doorway of the new study, surveying the devastation. "Bloody Hell," said Philip.

Portrait of a Lady

Moving house always means getting rid of unnecessary stuff, but in Philip's case there was very little in the way of accumulated tat. He only kept what was important, though I did sometimes wonder about the tea-stained coaster from the Isle of Wight that bore the legend:

Friendship

A friend sincere
is one who seeks to help
you in your life
To laugh away the hours
with you
and comfort you in
strife.

Imagine a flat square piece of polished plywood standing only just clear of a table surface by dint of four felt feet. A circle of cork stuck dead centre, inscribed with the words above, arranged geometrically so as to make the best use of its πr^2. The line endings used to drive me crazy.

Lord knows how Philip came by it; it was just always there, among the minimal impedimenta he carried with him from each address to the next, along with the wooden lid of a packing case for Hudson's Dry Soap, a section drawing he'd made of the north-east coast at Saltburn and his precious map of Ithaca.

And there was something else. A portrait of a lovely young woman with short blonde hair, her slim hands folded in her lap. Not a painting but a photograph, printed on canvas-textured paper in an antique gilded frame.

Philip was living in Whitby when we met. He was starting a new life. He had just given up both alcohol and cigarettes and was coping with the many stresses of the situation by employing complicated mind-games. He was effectively reinventing himself to correspond with his own criteria of human excellence. That was why he started lessons at a Dance Academy in Khyber Pass. His teacher was called Valerie and he fell hopelessly in love with her.

Valerie was an energetic, down-to-earth Yorkshire lass, happily married and devoted to dancing. Her dream was to own her own school. The first time I saw her she was working on a routine with a dozen children dressed as bees. Their ill-fitting costumes kept disappearing up their chubby bottoms in irritating wedgies which they fingered absent-mindedly as they jigged and giggled. She called them cheerfully to order, reminded them of what they were aiming for and started up the music. As the rhythm kicked in I could see the concentration and feel the aspiration as the image of a chorus-line communicated itself from their talented teacher.

Her encouragement of Philip was no different from what she offered to all her pupils but to him it was a lifeline and he held onto it very tightly. She became his muse. He wrote to me of his devotion to her and of his utter despair at having been unable to repay her patient tuition with a perfect rumba. During lessons he wore white cotton gloves as a gesture of propriety.

One cannot study European literature without coming across the concept of Courtly Love, the stories of the knight and his lady, whose relationship is pure and unsullied by commerce and sex. There is always a dream of eventual union but there are tests that must be passed, often imposed by the knight himself, conscious always of his ongoing unworthiness. This is how I saw them, Philip and Valerie, and I came to understand it through literary precedent.

Once upon a time there was a dance in the Spa Ballroom where Philip had taken me as a partner so as to avoid the stigma of the unattached man. Suddenly the gramophone stuttered and failed. Philip froze, then reddened, sharing Valerie's embarrassment. He leaped to his feet—"There's a problem..." and sped to her side to sort it out. Others more qualified to help had already assembled by the turntable but as he disappeared into the throng I saw Don Quixote riding to the rescue of the Lady Dulcinea. And that, I realised, made me his Sancho Panza, following at a distance on an overloaded donkey but always within call.

Philip engaged a local photographer to take the picture of Valerie, supposedly as a parting gift for her when he moved to Wales, but his own copy hung above his desk for the rest of his life. He wrote to her and sent her little gifts and she wrote back to him with her news and always remembered his birthday. She often apologised for her spelling and the mundanity of her letters, but she remained true to their friendship and I loved her for it.

Her picture hangs on my wall now, not exactly in pride of place but where I can see it from time to time. I will always be proud to have known Valerie, whose dancing feet trod softly on someone else's dream and who fine-tuned my definition of a Lady.

Homes and Gardens

The one and only rear window in Number 21 looked out on a small, flat garden, level with the upper floor. It had originally been part of the garden of Number 20, with access by stone steps from the yard and Philip had planted it and cherished it. He built himself a small summerhouse in the farthest corner, roofed with Clematis Tangutica whose summer sprawl of golden lanterns changed in autumn to a crust of white whiskery seedheads.

He planted three trees there; a rowan at the top of the steps, a crab apple by the boundary wall and a Juneberry, like a shrub on a stick, placed artfully at random in the rough lawn.

Philip loved this part of his garden best and used to call it *the parterre*. Before he became ill, whenever he went next door to daydream in Number 21, he would sit at the window and delight in the view from it. He told me he pretended he was looking at someone else's garden but I suspected he pretended he was someone else, looking at his own garden. Feelings of pride, I thought, rather than envy—but what's a deadly sin between friends?

When I found myself in charge of selling Number 20, I looked carefully at the plans, then drew a vertical line from the top of the garden to the place where the two houses joined. I was buggered if I'd let him give up his precious *parterre*. I had intended that we would also hold onto the right of way so we could still use the steps to get up there, but Philip refused, saying that nobody would buy the big house if it meant having us trailing past their downstairs windows unannounced.

So now, although Philip's precious space was safe, there was no easy access to it. The back door led into a narrow yard between the house and the high retaining wall of the garden but this had been roofed over with clear Perspex as a sort of storage area with another door at the end into the yard of Number 22. The only way to reach the garden was by means of a ladder that our pleasant neighbour let me keep by his back door.

But Philip could not manage the ladder. I would go up and carry out his bidding while he watched from the one small window at the back of the house. He would lean out and gesticulate instructively on days when he felt well but sometimes he had to sit down on the chair on the landing. Then I could only see the top half of his head, his homespun haircut, feisty eyebrows and sad eyes. That worried me. I strimmed and trimmed and wondered. How could I bring about the miracle that would stop him grieving for his garden while he was physically unable to get into it, like Alice down the rabbit hole?

The clue, it transpired, was in the question, though it took me a while to work it out.

Discussing Wittgenstein

As it happens, we did discuss Wittgenstein occasionally.

One of the things that exercised us greatly for a while was a discussion of his assertion that there can be no such thing as a private language. I thought that was daft. From the point of view of the individual, all language is private, since its use is completely subjective. To take that a step further, whether such a thing as a totally private language can exist depends wholly on one's definition of 'private'. We eventually let the matter rest, returning to tinker with it from time to time like a wooden puzzle. On one thing we were in complete agreement; since words themselves were so critical to Wittgenstein's arguments it was a shame he wrote them all in German, of which neither of us had more than a passing grasp.

One evening we sat together watching a television series we both enjoyed. *Star Trek—The Next Generation*. It was the episode called 'Darmok'. Captain Jean-Luc Picard is marooned on a hostile planet with a member of an alien race, who greets him with the words, "Darmok and Jilad at Tanagra." Because of the technological advances of the era he has no trouble understanding the words of his companion, but still hasn't a clue what he's actually saying. It transpires that the language the alien uses consists wholly of metaphorical allusions to the literature and mythology of his people. It is therefore unusable by Picard, who has to find a myth of his own to equate to the same situation—two very different people brought together by fate to face a situation that is destined to be the death of one of them. Picard chooses the Sumerian epic of Gilgamesh.

Philip howled with laughter. "How many trekkies will ever have read *that*?" I knew that the mindset of the *aficionado* would lead them to explore the idea. "Not yet, Oscar..." I began. He caught my eye and we concluded in unison, "...but they will, they will!"

Philip and Annie at Blaina? Indeed.

Wittgenstein, when trying to describe the mind, said it was like a beetle in a box. Everyone could open their own box and look at their own beetle, but nobody could open anybody else's box, so you had to take their beetle on trust.

Once, on a bad day, when Philip was trying to find something in his study, he muttered to himself, "Oh God, I must be losing my mind."

"You mean, your beetle's run away?" I asked.

"*Gorn!*" he said, striking a tragic attitude, "and never called me 'Mother'—will you help me look for it?"

"Aha—how will I know it if I see it?"

"It looks just like yours," he said. A moment's silence.

"Thank you," I said.

"I'll help you find it," I promised him solemnly, "and when we get it back in the box we'll make sure it doesn't get away again." We had segued seamlessly from Wittgenstein to Winnie-the-Pooh, who had no difficulty with the concept of a private language.

"Will you write 'Beetle' on the lid?" he asked. "Oh yes, very blackly" I assured him.

The Faraday Cage

It was a small hexagonal greenhouse, with a pointed roof like a wizard's hat. Green it was, with a painted metal framework that stood on a sextet of heavy duty paving stones to the left of the front door, effectively consuming half the area of the modest yard. Philip ordered it from a garden centre in Raglan and a man came with it to put it together *in situ.* He brought the paving stones, too. It was intended as a special place from which to look at the sky, an exclusive observatory within a few feet of the house.

The sky had always been a joy to Philip. The physicist in him exulted in the mysteries of atmospheric optics. He loved rainbows. He would stop the car and we would get out to look at a dramatic example of crepuscular rays, when a luminescent curtain falls from a shining slit in a dull sky. He would tell me that his mother always used to say it was 'the sun drawing water'. My own family had called it 'Jacob's ladder', but I never told him that, since to do so would have been eventually competitive. I adopted his expression instead. It was indisputably a many-splendoured thing.

Because of its grounded metal construction, Philip explained, the greenhouse was also a safe refuge from the dangers of electricity. Both of us had a lifelong love of thunderstorms. We would get up and go to the window, drawn by a flicker of lightning, counting like children: One— *elephant*, Two—*elephants* ...until the low rumble came from the demonstrated distance.

Now, at the first hint of a storm, we would take supplies outside. See us sitting in merry communion, fortified with cocoa and carrot-cake, raising a single finger to the worst excesses of the elements—*Blow winds and crack your cheeks!* It was in such moments of inspired silliness that we were truly us.

The Importance of the Corkboard

The cartoon on the cover of this book is one of the things that Philip pinned on the corkboard that hung on the kitchen wall. It is where we put the things that were momentarily important and kept those that became permanently significant.

"Look," he said as he skewered it with a map pin, "this is us." And it was. Bud Handelsman's drawing contrasted the absolute ordinariness of what was going on around us—the world wagging rhythmically in its prearranged progress, marked by little rituals and meteorological observations—with the bizarre specialness of what was being created behind our front door. They were them, but we were something else entirely. It was understood.

Some time later, doodling on the edge of something I was writing, I drew a mouse, arms raised in ecstasy, mouth open in a great cry of affirmation—'Hooray for us!' I cut it out and pinned it up without comment.

Throughout this special time, the corkboard stayed in its appointed place at the foot of the stairs, doing the odd jobs we gave it. Its basic shape lost under an accumulation of small memoranda, it lay flat against the panelling like a dead pangolin tacked to a shed door. Over the weeks pin-ups came and went. Crosswords that needed finishing, ideas that shimmered in and out of focus and jokes that were the better for being shared. But the Handelsman cartoon and the silly mouse were fixtures, curling aesthetically alongside the calendar with the obligations and the commitments and the days being ticked off one by one.

The Hawk and the Handsaw

It was while we were tarting up the bathroom that the thought occurred to me. Philip was sawing battens to support a new false ceiling and I was on tiptoes on the lavatory seat, making good the render on the rear wall, whence the old overflow pipe had been removed. I climbed down carefully. "Can I show you something?" I asked, choosing my moment so as not to interrupt a burst of zizzing. He sat down on the seat I had vacated and I set out to explain my little epiphany. "You and I," I began, "are both right-handed, are we not?" He nodded.

It had occurred to me, you see, that I, plastering, was plying the trowel with my right hand while the flat hawk holding the dollop of wet render was held in my left. He, however, had been steadying the battens across the edge of the bath with his left hand and wielding a small saw with his right. I laid down the trowel, picked up the saw and waved it aloft. "Look!" I said, "handsaw!" and then raising my left hand, which still held the empty tray, "hawk!"

"Hamlet!" he cried, getting my drift with evident delight. I carried on excitedly demonstrating that all that stuff we had been told by our English teachers, gleaned from dusty footnotes, about falconry metaphors and the putative 'heronsew' was but the retrospective maundering of the academic class. The groundlings would have got it in one — the man who can't tell a hawk from a handsaw simply doesn't know his right from his left. And thus, by intelligent extension, hawk and handsaw are but the Elizabethan equivalents of arse and elbow.

Philip seized cheerfully upon the idea. He agreed that, until these enlightened times, the people who devoted themselves to laying down the literary law had been more likely to train birds of prey than to plaster karzies and that, as art passed further into the purlieu of the artisan, many more such obvious conclusions would be drawn.

Later, in bed, he asked sleepily whether I considered that Shakespeare might have been the first to stumble upon the concept of dominant cerebral hemispheres. "Nah. Loada speculative bollocks," I replied, and settled my left hip into the curve between his arse and his elbow.

Letter to my Publisher

5th October 1998

(He had asked me to do some work with his local school on National Poetry Day and I had hoped to take Philip with me.)

Dear Harry,

A note in haste on Monday morning. Since we spoke, things have been up and down, as it were. Just as you were about to leave for your holiday, Philip had one of his episodes of acute anaemia and breathlessness and was admitted for blood transfusions and diuretic infusions and heroin injections and…

I thought the timing was excellent and hoped that it would 'last', so to speak, since he feels quite well for a while after these ministrations and he was looking forward to Calstock like an excited child. The tickets are in my handbag and it all seemed probable—but in the last day or so he has started to slip again and can't breathe. We've an appointment to see his consultant tomorrow but I am going to try to bring it forward to today.

Harry, it looks as though we won't be able to make it. If there's the ghost of a chance, I'll be there—perhaps without him if I can be sure he's safe and unafraid, but please look to the fallback position as I think we will need to call on it.

Oh, Harry, I've lain awake for the last two nights worrying and when Philip said 'soon we'll be in Cornwall' I thought my heart would break. It all seems such a huge mess and I'm so sorry. Please try to forgive me. I'm not usually the sort of person who lets people down but it looks as though this time I may have to.

Yours in utter wretchedness

Listening to Webern

Not that we ever did—listen to Webern, that is. I wonder whether there would have been a meeting of minds if we had.

We shared an overall preference for classical music, enjoyed many an opera together and held hands across vast acreages of orchestral work but radiating from that central nubbin were quite a few individual dendrites. Philip used Baroque music in his meditation sessions and I found much of it exhilarating, yet I couldn't listen to the Albinoni *Adagio* without laughing uncontrollably, as though at the death of Little Nell. And I never dared face the scorn he'd have poured on Meatloaf and Queen.

This was no revelation of a hitherto unsuspected side of his nature. He had always been a bully just as I had always been a victim and we had both had previous relationships where this had been an issue. We were older and wiser now. Most of the time our flaws balanced each other beautifully, but sometimes he would get violently angry with me, then insist that it was my miserable submissiveness that called up the demons and fed them, so that to have the temerity to suggest that his tantrum had caused my tears ... etc. It was a circle that had to be broken now and then.

"Paranoia," one of us would say, "is a survival trait." — (*cue laughter*). Philip had told me this once and now one or other of us would produce it like a wisp of silk from a prestidigitator's pocket and wave it when any argument arrived at an impasse. It was a grown-up equivalent of 'fainites'.

Philip loved to sing. He had a pleasant light baritone that, when he came to Wales, he tried to whittle into a tenor so as to sing in a local choir. It was a disaster. I remember his practising 'Fine Knacks for Ladies' hour after hour, squeezing his voice into an uncomfortable purée and forcing it into his sinuses as though by means of an icing syringe. It was all part of his search for a way of releasing the mystical inner creativity that he believed would change his life and make him happy. I searched constantly for a way to make him stumble on the discovery that his skill in innovative thinking and everyday improvisation, a delight to others that he took utterly for granted, was the very ore from which creativity is extracted.

'Horse 'n Box' was a simple example, though it occasionally drove me mad. He claimed that there was no tune written to which one could not sing the following: *Here is a horse and here is a box and there are the holes for its ears.* You had to throw scansion to the winds and sometimes repeat a phrase in juddering syncopation like a spaced-out rapper, but by and large it worked. The Toreador song from Carmen offered a particularly fine demonstration.

Once, after one of his occasional rages, he stumped around the kitchen in pan-clattering dudgeon, singing it at the top of his voice like a schoolboy showing the world he didn't care. This time, though, I didn't play the 'paranoia' card; instead I crept away leaving a large notice pinned to the corkboard. *In some cultures*, it informed him, *Horse n' Box is known as The Horse-vessel Song.* I heard the roar of laughter when he found it.

Caerleon College

As soon as he felt ready to chance his luck in social situations Philip enrolled at Caerleon College to undertake a Master's Degree in the Department of Archaeology. Because he was unable to move far without a wheelchair and occasionally needed nursing attention at short notice I was included in the placement as his care assistant. We became students again together and began learning about the relationship between the Romans and the Celts. It was a happy time despite the extraordinary circumstances and I was glad of the chance to study, albeit unofficially, a subject so close to my heart. We had both learned Latin at school and been captivated by this extraordinary society and the period that fell between the world it gradually superseded and that which eventually replaced it. In childhood we had both fantasised about it and played games of being there. The Celts, though, were still a bit of a mystery to both of us.

The building was not especially wheelchair-friendly but the students who formed the college were a different matter. So alive were they to the needs of the disabled elderly that our occasional forays along the corridors became a glorious, madcap progress. A couple of students would sprint ahead, barge open the double doors and then stand at attention, holding them open while I whizzed Philip through between them. He would wave his stick in the air, crying, "Bravo," and they would overtake and see to the next set of doors, unless other students further along had taken it upon themselves to hold them for us. They saw a woman pushing a bloke in a wheelchair and they did what came naturally. It was a joy.

At home we talked about this spontaneous behaviour and concluded that we were unusual in our attitude to it. Such cheerful goodwill is being rendered increasingly unnecessary by draconian legislation 'in favour' of the disabled and often downright forbidden by the Health and Safety lobby. Legally-imposed political correctness practically criminalises informal offers of help and the obviously disabled are thus becoming objects of fear and suspicion. Just as they were in less enlightened times.

The actual language of the learning was a particular delight. We cherished the specialist words peculiar to our subject and traded them happily within the group, like a coinage that had been specially struck for a small isolated civilisation. At home we incorporated them into our own verbal currency and sometimes we would use one to purchase a conspiratorial grin. We noticed one buzzword in particular. It turned up in almost every lecture and was never defined, the speaker always assuming we understood. Liminal. "What does it mean?" asked Philip. I said that to me it meant a period of stillness in a transient process. Standing on a threshold in front of an open door, committed to entry yet not quite ready to take the step, wiping one's feet and adjusting one's collar... "Well, yes—but what do *they* mean?" asked Philip. And we were discussing Wittgenstein again. "When I die," said Philip, "and you write the eulogy, you must be sure to use the word liminal, or my spirit won't rest." I said I would.

I learned a lot at Caerleon. I loved every minute and tiptoed with bated breath into many areas of archaeology that had hitherto been mysteries to me. Carbon dating, for instance, and the importance of C-transformation. I had a bit of trouble getting to grips with that. Apparently when one finds certain substances during an investigation, such as the examination of 'grave-goods' buried with the dead, the trained mind can extrapolate backwards to determine what they had been heretofore. I assumed that this would go on into the future and that new substances would lay down their own rules for the process. The thought somehow comforted me.

> *Full six feet deep thy father lies*
> *Of his bones are carbons made*
> *Cheap shoes and polyester ties*
> *Archaeologists upgrade*
> *Till they suffer a C-change*
> *Into something rich and strange.*
> *Hourly they argue his home and habit*
> *Hark! Now I hear them...rabbit, rabbit...*

Sometimes the speaker would leave us behind a bit and the notional rabbit became an acknowledgement of the occasional obscurity created by experts who find themselves preaching to the genuinely unconverted. Usually we asked for clarification but if Philip felt he was alone in losing his grasp of an argument, he would doodle a puzzled animal on the edge of his notepad and call my attention to it with a flourish of his eyebrows. I would reply discreetly, in kind, usually acknowledging an equal confusion. On such occasions we were like naughty children passing notes in class, but we would take the questions home with us and find the answers later. We both took the studies seriously and we didn't miss a single one of the special lectures right up to the day Philip died.

However, things were not always easy for a disabled student and his supernumerary carer. One lecture in particular proved especially problematic. Philip's wheelchair was placed at a right angle to the far end of the front row and since there was no spare seat I perched on a desk beside him. It was hellish hot and the edge of the desk threatened to cut off the blood supply to my lower legs. We were attending a lecture entitled *Roman Invasion: Conflict or Consensus?* I kept repeating it in my head and playing it surreptitiously on the

41

desk with the tips of my fingers; the sound of it pleased me hugely, echoing as it did the hendecasyllabic music in the poetry of Catullus. I wondered if this was deliberate. I rather hoped so, but nobody else mentioned it and I didn't dare ask, just in case. I hid behind my role of carer, listening hard for all I was worth. That, it transpired, was all either of us could do since the visiting academic stood with his back to us, waving wildly like a charismatic conductor and effectively obscuring the flipchart. In an attempt to take my mind off my deadening legs, I pretended I *was* Catullus, scribing notes, recreating the picture that was being drawn by the gesticulating lecturer…

> *…Here comes Claudius, sailing up the Solent*
> *(Not too fast on account of the elephants)*
> *All dressed up in his people-pleasing purple*
> *Out on deck with the shiny-looking soldiers*
> *Standing straight as his gammy leg will let him,*
> *Face all stretched with the effort of his trying*
> *Not to laugh at the acrobatic pirates…*

I loved the acrobatic pirates. The lecturer insisted that they were germane to his argument for a degree of collaboration between the invading forces and the would-be client kings. I nudged Philip and showed him the pirate poem; he replied with a sketch of a shifty-looking fellow swinging from the rigging with a dagger between his teeth. When I later got a look at one of the other students' notes, I glumly observed that they were actually 'Atrebatic pilots'. But by then it was too late.

Number 8

Seven years before Philip fell ill, while he was still living in busy bachelorhood in the big house at Number 20 and I was visiting on a regular basis, I bought Number 8. It was an old stone terraced cottage further down the road, two up, two down and derelict. When I first saw it, it was full of other people's bicycles, brick rubble and unfeasible amounts of sunshine. It streamed in through the old sash windows at the front until mid-day, whereupon it changed tack and trickled more decorously down the stone steps that led up to the rotten frame of the absent back door. It was love at first sight and I paid cash for it. I undertook the restoration myself using Philip as a sort of guru. To some extent this equated to the blind leading the blind, but Number 8 was a forgiving mistress and anyway Philip was the only person I hoped to impress.

The neighbours were curious about the nature of our relationship. One of them said once that it must be convenient to be able to have a row, slam the door and walk out in my slippers without having to lose face by stopping to change. Fishing, as it were. I did not take the bait.

When the Bright Young Things bought Number 20 and we began to live together in Number 21, I never for a moment considered selling Number 8. This was my own place. Even when I married Philip and took up residence as his wife, I thought of Number 8 as mine, never 'ours'.

I visited it every day. My dogs lived there. And Trevor, the ageing cat that had issued forth unbidden from the ginger kitten Philip had bought me in Marlborough. I remember the deliberately quaint shopping precinct where we saw the advertisement and Philip responding to my enthusiasm like the wicked Wickham hoping to seduce Lydia Bennet with a trinket. I didn't tell him that, but thought of it whenever I fingered the orange dome of Trevor's head or the little fistfuls of baked beans that formed the underneaths of his feet.

At Number 21 we lived beyond our limited means and juggled Philip's credit cards like plates on sticks. I knew that when he died everything we shared would disappear and that I'd have to sort out the mess. But for all that, when the men from the Hong Kong and Shanghai Bank came to discuss finances and suggested I might use my property as security for a further loan, I refused. I still feel guilty about that.

Act of Worship

My own house is a holy place for my purposes;
my pottering in it is a sort of prayer.

By making the effort to come here
I have turned my back on all the fidgety busyness
of the sticky world I've spun around myself, its plan
no longer entirely recognisable. A sad old spider
whose knitting feet fumble forgotten patterns,
I wander unwatched, forgiving myself slowly.

Forgiving myself for the terrible lapse of taste
That put the stained glass in the door—*my dear, so thirties!*
Forgiving the blowsy bevels because of the rainbows
coincidentally blessing the dizzy dust.

Becoming slowly glad, recalling the slick, sweet taste
of the safety that lives in the dark behind closed doors.
The dear curves of the squat little armchair, the benison
bestowed unconditionally on the backs of bare knees
by the kiss of uncut moquette.

These are my own things. Nobody else would want them,
yet among them I can give thanks; here I can praise.
I am home again, after a long time; a lapsed Catholic
absentmindedly making all the appropriate gestures,
prompted by long-forgotten habit.

For it feels like being in church, the afternoon ending
in a fine, slow, aromatic contemplation,
my old cat limp in my lap like a Sunday glove.

The Fierce Bad Rabbit

Another of the creatures I kept at Number 8 was a small black-and-white rabbit. It had belonged to a family that had moved away and left it behind since it was of a particularly fractious disposition. It chased cats and bit children. I think it came with a name but Philip always referred to it as the Fierce Bad Rabbit and so it—she—became.

I used to tell stories about her. I'd come back after a visit to the creatures and Philip would hear me come in. "What's the Fierce Bad Rabbit been up to?" he would ask, and I would tell bizarre lies to make him laugh.

There was still no easy way to get Philip into the back garden. As he got frailer I decided on an experiment. One day I brought the Fierce Bad Rabbit back to Number 21 and set up a home for her under the upstairs window where Philip could peer out at her when she was let loose in the *parterre.*

Her escape attempts were a constant source of fascination. She tunnelled furiously—she could disappear in minutes from a standing start. She could run up rough walls like a squirrel and used shadows to disguise her reconnaissance of the perimeter fence. Her efforts to evade capture at night and my clumsy attempts to outwit her provided even more innocent merriment.

Philip suggested that she needed company and I found Mister Brown at a rabbit rescue centre in the Rhondda. He was a big, easygoing fellow and it didn't take long for him to ingratiate himself with herself, so to speak. Nonetheless, I had him neutered on arrival—the Fierce Bad Rabbit had had young once and eaten them all.

After a while someone gave us some guinea pigs. They too became a source of amusement in the guise of a subject of study. On fine days when we could keep an eye on them, they would be let out on their own to run around the front garden. Because Philip couldn't see them from his chair unless they were well away from the house, I put a mirror up against the far wall. It was large and convex and it magnified and distorted them slightly, so that when Philip looked out of the window to see what they were up to they were magically transformed into displaced capybara going about their mysterious business among the shadows of an impenetrable rainforest. Which was exactly what I had had in mind.

I had my misgivings, of course. I sometimes saw myself dragging this clear-sighted physicist down into a warped world of childish fantasy and hated myself for dangling a rose-tinted gauze over the unalterable backdrop. *Twee*, I hissed at myself sometimes, and threatened my throat with two fingers.

Nevertheless, this Beatrix Potter world-within-a-world had its moments of enchantment. One evening we stood open-mouthed gazing upwards as the Fierce Bad Rabbit, oblivious and inspired, put on a Prima Donna performance in honour of the setting sun. With a pattering like leathery rain she danced on the transparent roof of the outhouse, leaping and spinning and settling at last into a squatting posture that put one in mind of a naughty netsuke—the kneeling geisha, decorously robed, who exposes everything when seen from underneath.

A Physical Relationship

Just remember this; love isn't sex
But the dreary things you do for the people you love

U A Fanthorpe: *Mother Scrubbing the Floor*

The official purpose of marriage is to sanctify sexual relations and place them firmly within the context of Christian living. Marriage is a sacrament that consecrates copulation and the subsequent production of issue on behalf of the Church. I, at the age of fifty-eight, had entered into marriage with a dying man whom I knew to be impotent. Was our relationship, then, a double abomination in the sight of the Lord? I don't think so.

Philip described the condition of celibacy as 'a higher plane' and I respected that, while keeping to myself the knowledge that physical contact in the form of intimate care can go a long way towards sexual fulfilment. Probably because I was ashamed of it, what with the higher plane and all.

I wondered, though, about nurses and the sub-cultural myths about their heightened sexuality, which must have come from somewhere—*Ooh, Matron!*—and I thought about field hospitals and nuns and amused myself greatly with concepts of the holy war and the holy whore. Thought, after all, is free.

And I remembered an AGM of the Samaritans, where a group of women walked out on Chad Varah when he suggested that the fierce and physical bond between mother and child had a sexual element. I had thought everyone knew that. The woman who was sharing my room was so appalled by the idea that she sobbed uncontrollably in my arms for some considerable time while I stroked her hair and explained, carefully, my own vision of the overall acceptability of humanity with all its wonderful conundrums. When she stopped crying she held me very tight for while before extricating her face from the damp patch between my breasts and thanking me with a kiss. I made no comment on that, but wondered whether, in the circumstances, I could consider it a job well done.

We discussed most things, Philip and I, including sex, albeit at the level of principle. Sometimes we wondered mutually about gender and how it affected worldview. Philip said that he felt that he ought to be more in touch with his feminine side, though he clearly didn't use me as a yardstick in his aspirations. I agreed that he should. He was a truly exceptional human being and the feminine side of his nature was no stranger to me. I cherished it already and so, I hoped, would he.

One day we happened to be talking about gods and the nature of power. In all mythologies the senior deity could demand sexual subservience from all sorts of mortals and therein we suspected an interesting insight. Without a moment's hesitation we plunged after it like a pair of ferrets.

Philip was interested in the significance of Zeus's decision to snatch Ganymede in the form of an eagle and to possess Leda in the persona of a swan. "Matter of equipment," I opined. "He needed a grabbing mechanism to airlift Ganymede from Ida to Olympus, whereas he saw to Leda on-site, as it were."

"Could it be," Philip wondered, "that the master of all things understood that a woman would be more readily seduced by beauty than by cruelty, her soft thighs more easily parted by cool webs than by raptorial claws?"

"More likely," I replied, wondering how I knew and why I felt the need to mention it, "it's because, had he become an eagle, he would have had to content himself with a perfunctory cloacal kiss, whereas the swan is the only bird that has a penis."

"Good Lord," said Philip, genuinely interested, "is that true?" I replied with an emphatic *mmm*, although I knew better. I crossed my fingers and added silently, "up to a point."

There is another bird similarly equipped but I did not choose to bring it into the discussion. Later I lay grinning in the dark. The whole notion of *Leda and the Duck* was just too delicious to share until I had explored it on my own for a while. What was it that the poet F W Harvey wrote on a bad day in Holzminden prison...*From troubles of the world...*?

Sleeping Together

'To sleep with' has become a euphemism
For fucking, humping, shagging, or whatever
Leads to orgasm, to the spurt of jism
That signals 'tools down' for the jobbing lover.
Sleeping with someone is an act of love—
Another phrase that raises nudge and wink
When it is innocently spoken of—
Though not erotic as the dullards think.
Sleeping is quiet time for private study;
A heaven-given opportunity
Of cherishing another human body
In all its perilous proximity,
Its promontories and its recesses,
The busy music of its processes.

Mixmaster b'long Jesus Christ

As Philip's bodily systems began to fail he was subject to dramatic swings of temperature. We bought two new things to help cope with this. One was a dual-control electric blanket and the other was a ceiling fan. The blanket was just a blanket but the fan was a glorious gold affair that was screwed to the wooden ceiling and drooped above the bed like an Amazon's tit. Attached to its nipple were two pairs of opalescent glass wings that spun like a dragonfly in agony or ecstasy according to whether you pulled once or twice on the cord that hung between us over the bed.

It was both hideous and fascinating. At its slower speed it whumped rhythmically, fostering an impression of weary subservience, like a faithful punkah-wallah, but when urged to go faster it flew round effortlessly like rotor blades on a gimbal. When it was first installed, Philip said that it was an autogyro that would lift us aloft and take us anywhere we wanted to go.

"Do you remember what they call such things in Papua New Guinea?" he asked.

"Mixmaster b'long Jesus Christ," I replied.

"Just testing," he grinned.

As if I could forget. 'Autogyro' was one of the words on which we could never agree. Philip pronounced it with a hard 'g' and I with a soft one. It was surprising how often it came up in conversation. Secret, solitary flight had been a childhood daydream of Philip's and this mechanism was how he had imagined himself achieving it. I could happily spell the word with a 'y' or an 'i' but could not bring myself to terms with his way of saying it. So he said it a lot, just to irritate me, and I argued every time, citing the softening effect of vowels and using Yeats as my yardstick, while he called upon Lewis Carroll. Thus, when we heard the perfect phrase allegedly coined by the unsophisticated natives of a backward culture, we adopted it at once.

Now Philip would ask "Mixmaster?" and I would say "If you like" and one of us would pull the cord and set it a-going. Sometimes he would say, "Where shall we fly off to?" and that 'we' pleased me, though I never made a point of saying so.

Now and again we made plans for real journeys but most of them had to be cancelled. One was a cut-price city-break in Honfleur. A brochure came through the door with a picture that seduced us instantly; a flower-decked quayside, whereon a vintage bicycle leaned artlessly against ancient railings, its basket overflowing with carnations. We discussed and investigated but the timing was against us. The date came too suddenly and I hoped he had forgotten. During the evening he said simply, "Pity about Honfleur."

I fell asleep sad and awoke smiling at the cunning plan that had formed in my imagination. I attended to Philip and slipped out to Number 8 to see to the dogs. On the way I went to the shed and got out my bike, an ancient Pashley Princess with a skirt-guard and a basket and an in-your-face *ding-dong* bell. I hadn't ridden it since Philip came out of hospital and the tyres were flat. *But only on the bottom,* I told myself and pushed it awkwardly along the road.

I looked for flowers to put in the basket. Carnations were a nonstarter and there wasn't really enough of anything else to justify plundering in the sort of quantities I had envisaged. Philip and I always avoided cutting precious flowers on principle, but in the derelict garden of Number 9 there was a prodigious crop of Rosebay Willow Herb, the opportunist invader of waste places, which had flower-spikes in such quantity as I had not seen since... Hickling! Oh, when the Lord don't come, he sends.

Years ago, when our relationship was very new, it almost foundered on a disastrous camping holiday in Norfolk. I was trying far too hard and in consequence did nothing right. Later I wrote him a poem about it:

> No, I don't remember an inn, beloved;
> I dimly recall a tent
> And the slow, sad sighs
> When I tripped on the guys
> And my wondering what it all meant.
> And the tears and the fears
> Of the first time in years
> That I'd been on my own with a bloke
> And the tedding and the spreading
> Of the polyester bedding
> And the tea that tasted of the smoke...

We had trudged hopelessly round a nature reserve on Hickling Broad. Philip insisted on walking sternly ahead of me, not speaking, clapping his binoculars occasionally to his eyes, waving me back with an irritated shushing motion and, by some sympathetic miracle, failing to see a single living creature among the great plantations of Willow Herb. Over the years the incident had been transformed from a bone of contention to a shared grin. It was part of our Norfolk Experience, as was the gratitude with which I had embraced the comfort of my own home after the strain of the holiday. Like the Pedlar of Swaffham, as I later explained.

And that was the message of the armfuls of Willow Herb in the basket of the vintage bicycle that I leaned artlessly against the wall of the front garden before I went back in to get the breakfast on the table and call Philip down to share it.

I was hiding in the larder when he came into the room, pulled up the blind and caught sight of the bicycle. After a few moments I went and stood beside him. He put his arm round my shoulders. "Once more into the breach, dear friend," he misquoted, softly.

UWE

You pronounce it *yoo-ee*, like an Australian's greeting across a considerable distance or an apocryphal nephew of Donald Duck.

I was already teaching one day a week in the School of English, Communication and Philosophy at Cardiff University, Undergraduate Creative Writing in the morning and a specialist Poetry group in the afternoon. The money came in handy and the change of scene gave a useful perspective on what was happening at home. This contract, though, was coming to an end and I had spotted a vacancy for a visiting writer at UWE—the University of the West of England. In Bristol.

I applied and was appointed. I would be working one day a week, teaching creative writing to two groups of students and supporting them in preparing a portfolio as part of their degree. I would also give occasional lectures and presentations and be generally available as an accessible working writer. They gave me a sunny office on the exquisite St Matthias campus in Fishponds and paid me generously. It was unquestionably a good idea. However, this didn't make it easy to accomplish.

Philip was encouraging and insisted that he would be perfectly happy without me on Wednesdays, but I worried constantly. I would help him to wash and give him breakfast, but he was usually still in bed when I left the house.

He had refused to have a telephone installed upstairs and once or twice, as he grew less agile, he had stumbled in an effort to reach the one in the kitchen. I dreaded the thought that he might do so while I was away but did not tell him so. Instead, I subscribed to BT's answering service. Philip knew of the innovation and I explained that there'd now be no need to rush to the phone, but I knew that wouldn't stop him. So I kept to myself the knowledge that I had remote access to the system and could thereby institute a cunning wheeze to ensure that the telephone would never ring while he was upstairs.

It worked like this. Before I left the house I pressed the buttons that would make the service pick up immediately without ringing. I arranged with Philip that he would call me during the morning, which he couldn't do till he was safely downstairs. After he had done so I would phone home without triggering a sound and change the response to the longest possible delay. It was both a guilty little secret and the nearest I could get to cherishing him *in absentia.*

The Wet Sandwich

Philip loved to surprise me with unusual food. One Wednesday he called to me as I came in after work. "Come straight through. I've made us a sandwich." I did, and indeed he had, though it took me a while to come to terms with it. What he brought to the table was a shapeless parcel, wrapped in foil, about the size and weight of a dead squirrel. "It's a new thing," he said proudly, "a wet sandwich."

It was certainly new to me. It was, he said, full of Mediterranean vegetables and as he sawed it in half it oozed olive oil and a melange of organic juices. I was horrified. It was a negation of years of searching for a way to stop salad sandwiches going soggy. It was a palpable abuse of a half-decent demi-baguette. "Is it supposed to do that?" I asked, hoping to express interest rather than distaste.

He showed me the recipe. It turned out it was not so much an innovation as a regional speciality. It is known as 'Pan Bagna' which is Provençal for 'soggy bread'. No pretensions there, then. I bit into the cut edge, clinging with both hands to the free end lest any of the flaccid contents should make a break for freedom. It dripped on my bosom and I lost a bit of aubergine, but it didn't taste at all bad. I caught Philip's eye and gave an appreciative grunt.

Soon the only things left on the table were one ball of screwed-up foil, two empty glasses and four elbows. We discussed the meal in a sort of retrospective Grace. Philip was glad he had made the experiment and I was glad I had taken up the challenge. I confessed my original misgivings and he forgave me, conceding that many comestibles enjoyed by some are viewed with suspicion by others and we amused ourselves looking for examples.

We considered the Bedfordshire clanger. We both knew of it as a sort of suet-crusted pasty, savoury at one end and sweet the other, that the wives of agricultural workers cooked for their men to take down to the fields. Neither of us, though, had ever eaten one. Philip because he didn't quite fancy the idea of conflating contrasts and I because it posed a question of etiquette that I could not answer. What, I wondered, did one do with the little bridge of pastry that separated the two? We imagined it as a bit of necessary gristle, Janus-faced at the junction, dunked in both gravy and jam. Did one spit it decorously like a prune-stone or hoy it boldly into the hedgerow for the birds? Philip said it was probably considered locally to be the best bit, offered to Luton dinner-guests like a sheep's eye at a Bedouin feast.

I fell silent, thinking. In art, life and cuisine, it takes courage to confront one's expectations. I decided that one day I would make a clanger and, after we had shared both ends, we would draw lots for the little mystery in the middle. Only then would we know for sure.

As Dean Swift once observed, "he was a bold man that first eat an oyster."

Great Expectations

Philip and I slowly realised, as we explored the system from within, that people expect too much of health professionals. Now that healthcare is regarded as a business, different criteria are used to judge its success. In a world where greed has replaced aspiration, the chance of proving someone wrong and profiting from it is presented as a legitimate perk. This is very sad.

On one of our follow-up visits to Mr. D, I took with me a copy of the poetry collection wherein he was first mentioned as 'The Italian Surgeon'. I had been horrified to discover, too late, that he was Maltese. He might well have found that deeply insulting and I had got books from the library to research his native language so that I could use it to write a simple dedication in the volume. Watching his face as he opened the book and read what I had written was like watching a sunrise. A slight stiffening, a small silence and a slow pink suffusion of pleasure that drew smiles from both of us as we sat across the desk and felt the relationship shifting subtly, as though a mist had lifted.

Most of the subsequent conversation has disappeared from my memory; I recall only that it was easy and covered subjects other than disease and death. During it, Mr. D confided that he had thought a great deal about Philip over the previous few months. He said he regretted that he had not followed his instinct during the second operation and used a different method of closure. Surrounded by students, he had chosen to employ the latest, well-researched technique but had often thought since that old-fashioned deep-tension sutures might have prevented the subsequent breakdown of the wound.

I heard myself as if from a great distance. "But, sir," I said, casual as you please, "if the deterioration began in the underlying tissues and the stitches had not allowed the septic material to escape, might there not have been a risk of anaphylactic shock?"

I have no idea where that came from. I made it up. It was probably complete bollocks, but I had no doubt that it was the right thing to say. Philip's hand slid across and rested on my knee. Mr. D lowered his head for a moment, then looked up and smiled. Something very important was mutually understood and truth had nothing to do with it.

Blowing Tanks

This was what Philip came to call the occasional mechanical passing of the accumulated wind in the plastic bag that had replaced his rectum.

While we were still living in the hospital I asked one of the doctors whether such emissions were still technically farts, since they did not proceed from an anus. He said it had never occurred to him and I was led to wondering once again about the workings of my mind. It mattered to me that there should be a correct term for these cheerful bodily functions.

We decided that, since their early provenance and ultimate nature remained unchanged they were still farts when they left the stoma, but became a kind of gaseous ballast thereafter. They stayed trapped in the bag close to his body, like the malevolent gales that Aeolus gave to Odysseus, so as to keep them from doing harm while the West wind, breath of his own autumnal being, steered him safely home.

But, like the Aeolian troublemakers, these naughty breezes had to be let out sooner or later. Philip developed a technique of standing outside on the front doorstep, sliding the clip off the end of the bag and squeezing out the gas, lifting it upwards the while, so that anything more solid should not escape by accident.

One day I arrived back with groceries and observed this ritual at a slight distance. What I saw was profoundly disturbing and I hastened to point this out to him. "Do be careful when blowing tanks," I said. "Think how it appears to a casual observer. An elderly gentleman facing the public highway, adjusting his nether garments to produce a pink, limber thing which he then holds aloft, stroking slowly from root to tip, as it were, with a look of evident relief."

I was actually quite serious but he was unexpectedly offended by the implication. He said angrily that only I would have thought of such a thing and that nobody else would ever make that obscene assumption. Near to tears, I reminded him of the Thirsk lorry-driver, making adjustments at the rear of his wagon with a beech-hafted claw-hammer stuck in his belt, who was reported for indecent exposure by a passing woman and was required to demonstrate his defence in the dock. "Oh, change the subject!" he growled hatefully and slammed the door in my face.

I withdrew into the Faraday cage and cried for some considerable time until the penny dropped. It dropped like a coin in a see-through charity box, clattering past self-pity, self-righteousness and self-justification till it landed and spun to a tipsy collapse in a puddle of self-awareness. It was my fault—I had done it again. My attempt at broad comedy had misfired badly and I had hit him amidships with a gratuitous paradiddle on my boom-boom drum.

I was sorry, but that wouldn't mend it. To say so would be to dwell on his vulnerability and make the hurt greater. For a while I woke daily to the memory of what I had done, but in time I forgave myself. And Philip never blew tanks on the doorstep again.

Affairs of the Heart

Since his discharge, Philip had been attending two sets of outpatient clinics, surgical and medical, but his occasional emergencies were almost exclusively within the bailiwick of the cardiology team who had fought so hard for him while he was in the hospital.

Kidney failure, atrial fibrillation, fluid retention, anaemia —episodes of all these triggered sudden brief re-admissions, and in between we went happily to see the remarkable doctors, looking forward to each appointment as though to a meeting with friends. Communication was easy and we laughed a lot. One of the doctors declared, "You two are *stars!*" and for a moment the tired old man and his terrified wife felt that it was so.

Having been tongue-tied once when Philip was asked a question and expected me to answer it for him, I began taking an up-to-date record of his medications and their dosages and frequencies. It was an impressive list that changed and grew. Dr D would spin round in his chair when we went in and stretch his hand out for it with a broad, appreciative smile. When eventually it stayed the same for three visits on the trot he raised his eyebrows and declared, "Well, old chap, it looks as though we've finally found the right combination. I only wish it hadn't taken us so long." Philip reached for his hand and shook it warmly. "I'm eternally grateful to you for persisting with the search," he said.

We left the clinic on a high. "I always feel better for coming here," I said to Philip.

"Does your heart good, doesn't it," he replied, with a grin.

Grand Days Out

Philip was still able to drive, though only for short distances. He grew anxious, though, that I should not refuse invitations to read and perform. Although I simply declined some of them without ever telling him, it made sense to accept the more possible ones and to go there together since it was a way of including him in my other life and he was still largely dependent on me for his everyday care. Up to a point I could draw on my experience of travelling with children and the need to carry the makings of the mother-magic that covers all possible disasters. Now, though, there were additional complications of wheelchair provision and emergency toilet access that became more problematic as time went on. Venturing long distances was an act of faith. We would set off like Chesterton's merry drunkards, confident that would get there anyhow — or, if not, that we would get somewhere somehow. And like them we awoke, more often than not, among roses.

We started with a glass of wine outside the George Hotel
For there I had a job to do and hoped to do it well
And afterwards we settled down and sank another one
To celebrate our bravery and toast a job well done.
We tottered to the Tally-ho! and happily to bed
The day we went to Hatherleigh by way of Holyhead.

The Company of Poets had invited me to read.
The fee that they were offering was generous indeed
But Devil take the money and secrete it in his store —
There are too many other things that matter so much more;
The powers that be applauded me and took great care of you
The day we went to Dartington by way of Timbuktu.

When once I had been summoned to receive a modest prize
We trundled off at sparrow-fart with angst behind our eyes.
I took the cheque and ate the lunch you felt too ill to share,
Then joined the march to Housman's church and wished that you
                                                    were there.
But you were at the window and you waved and blew a kiss
The day we went to Ludlow by way of Dungeness.

Though travelling is difficult and distance is a curse
We know it's worth the effort and we know it could be worse.
We knew what we were in for when they made us man and wife
And bumbling through, for me and you, is now a way of life
And there'll be many sights to see and many thoughts to share
Before we get to you know what by way of God knows where.

Letter to my Publisher

3rd July 1999

(At the launch of my second collection in June, Harry had invited me to take part in the first Peterloo Poetry Festival; Philip was included in the invitation.)

Dear Harry,

This is the letter I intended to write the minute I got home after the book launch and had to shelve because of one of Philip's sudden relapses.

However, he is back home again and we are embarking on the jolly game of anticoagulants where we have to go to the hospital on alternate days to have them check his clotting factor. Presumably when they have thinned his vital fluids down far enough I shall at last be in a position of supreme power—I'll only have to bite his arse and he'll bleed to death. What fun!

Still, he's back home and feeling fairly well so I can pick up where I left off and say what I want to say, which is to repeat formally what I said in a hurry on the phone: thank you.

We've decided to make the September doings in Calstock a mini-holiday so could you look into the possibilities of B&B accommodation for two for the whole Festival and an extra day either side of it. I'll send a deposit to secure the booking. Nothing palatial—just so Philip can potter about on the (relatively) flat when left to his own devices and I can find my way back to it pissed.

I look forward to hearing from you and to seeing you again in September. Thank you again for a very special day.

Eclipse

Did I tell you about the Wild Garden? While things were good and Philip was still immortal, he bought a piece of land that lay alongside Number 20. It had belonged to a monumental mason and consisted of the demolished remains and overgrown gardens of the two missing houses in the row, Numbers 18 and 19. Here and there among the brambles lay half-finished memorials. Some had obvious typographical errors proving that such small oversights can happen to anybody and that stonemasons pay a higher price for them than most, some seemed perfect but had just never been installed, perhaps due to changes of mind or unforeseen inelasticities of budget. We cleared the overgrowth around them and set them right-way-up as part of the garden, a weird coming-together of Christian observance and Zen happenstance.

We planted trees. Rowans and birches thrived cheerfully beside the alders that grew unbidden. A lusty hornbeam raised itself head and shoulders above a sickly London plane that almost died. Among all these young hopefuls Philip built a bird-watching hut where he spent hours looking and drawing. I gave him an oak for his sixty-fifth birthday, telling him it was the acorn he would have planted in his youth if he had thought of it in time. It settled in alongside an ash that was there already and they touched branches companionably beside the huge landscaped pond that housed fish and frogs and dragonflies and the solitary Great Diving Beetle that lurked and pounced beneath the innocent surface.

Now that his health was failing the wild garden became a special consolation and on the day of the total eclipse we took food and drink and curiosity and settled on camping chairs under the trees by the water to await the mystical performance. We didn't talk much, just watched and thought and smiled at one another from time to time.

I remembered our first trip to France, not long after we met. A disastrous camping experience near St Coulomb, where Philip went for long walks on the beach at sunset hoping to catch a glimpse of the mysterious green flash, an example of atmospheric optics that had eluded him all his life. He insisted on going alone. I knew that this was all part of his search for that mystical insight into everything that he felt was only just out of reach and I tried hard to understand. Even so I felt abandoned as I wandered round the campsite by myself or climbed the rocks above the Plage des Chevrets, trying not to look at the horizon in case I saw the flash myself by accident; not as well, but instead. I could not help wondering why on earth he had invited me to come with him.

Now though, we were together with no need for phatic chuntering or constant comparison of notes. We used the water's surface to watch the sky and now and then I stole a glance at Philip, watching him watching. There were questions I longed to ask but I knew that there were some things that he still treasured to himself, as we all do. And if I loved him I would have to let them go. So I did.

The Shadow of the Moon

'Oh, what the hell' we said, and did the thing
Without protection. Risky undertaking.
With our bare eyes we watched the sun's eclipse
Reflected in the surface of the pond.

Wet-blanket clouds had shackled its full power;
It lay in the water, Achilles' shield,
Dull, sunken silver. Then a dozen orfe —
Pond-swallows – gurgitated centre-stage
Chasing a drift of midges, shattering
The picture beyond mere representation —
Matisse — Cézanne — and all the broken light
Shimmered into a glorious, soundless noise.

I turned to you to share the glee, and saw
The first shadow of pain crossing your face.
You hid it well. No sooner there than gone.

The cloud lifted. The sun was back again.
The orfe retreated into the dark place
Under the lilies. Something had ended.
Something had begun.

Letter to my Publisher

16th August 1999
(As plans firmed up for our trip to Cornwall)

Dear Harry,

What Larks! Thanks for booking us into such perfect accommodation. How nice, too, to be sharing the digs with Gabriel *(Fitzmaurice)*. I was talking to him on the phone last week and he sounds as excited as I am.

Our plans so far fit in wondrously with yours. We are coming on the Thursday to save rush and are booked into a hotel in Plymouth for Thursday night. The cunning plan at the moment is to come up to Calstock on the boat (…the barge she sat in etc.) on Friday, arriving around lunchtime, so the Tamar Inn would have been our first stop anyway!

Should the boat prove All Too Difficult (inadequate stowage, need for breeches buoy etc.) we'll get a train, but no need to meet us if the slope is *down* as we will have a wheelchair with us (…*wheeeee!*) therefore the only problems may be *uppards*, as it were, and we can sort those out when we come to them.

And it gets better. Remember last October? I had bought train tickets for our aborted visit and although in theory I could have got a refund I didn't have the heart at the time. Last week I threw myself on the mercy of Wales and West Trains and they said they'd swap the unused tickets for travel vouchers to cover the forthcoming trip—so no expenses claim!

Philip is hugely enthusiastic, planning white-knuckle wheelchair rides round the Hoe and pink gins in the hotel bar so as to appear Naval. I am creeping about among all his various specialists, trying to get everything done to ensure he is really well for the holiday while giving the appearance of nonchalance. It struck me that it's rather like getting a prize beast to an agricultural show in the best possible condition; panicking lest he lose form or peak too early. Still, *toujours gai.*

See you in September.

To The Peterloo Festival…

The Imperial Hotel, as we had twigged from the tone of the brochure, had a sort of Naval theme underpinning its ambience. They had given us a ground floor room because of the wheelchair. Philip, making a jolly of it, said that I should refer to him as The Commander and hint at a war wound when he was out of earshot.

Plymouth was an adventure. It was our first long-distance foray with the wheelchair and I soon realised that in certain circumstances it was a dangerous conveyance. The hotel was on a steep slope and the weather was particularly hot. I found that my sweaty palms had little grip on the plastic handles and the brake, which was operated by foot from behind, was designed only to hold the chair still on the flat during loading and disembarkation procedures. It could not be used to slow the downhill progress of the occupied chair. The journey into town began with a steep trundle down Lockyer Street and a sharp right onto Notte Street so I insisted on doing the first bit backwards. Philip couldn't see the need but I explained that the only alternative was to ask the hotel to lend him an anchor that he could lob overboard if he felt that the chair was gaining speed and that I was no longer attached to it.

Plymouth is a lovely city and we explored it happily. We found Phoenix Wharf where the boats set off for trips up the Tamar and booked our tickets for Calstock the following day. Then we had a late lunch in a lovely Italian restaurant on Southside Street and were so preoccupied with our meal and each other's company that we failed to notice that we were now the only customers. We were puzzled when the waiter who came to ask if we would like coffee seemed to be a very small boy. The restaurant, it transpired, had been closed for some time. All the other diners had left. The host, who had been expected to pick up his son from school, had rung his wife to ask her to collect him on her way to work and drop him off at the restaurant, where he was now proudly helping his dad. We learned all this from the smiling host who joined us at our table, brushing off our shamefaced apologies with Neapolitan grace. We were no longer his customers but his guests. I was quite sure that this would prove to be the highlight of our visit but in this I was deceived.

That evening we went for a stroll around the Barbican. As I was negotiating the cobbles, with Philip rising to the wheelchair's uncomfortable trot, a tall shadow detached itself from the gathering dusk and fell in alongside ours. "Please— I help you?" I turned to see a mighty man with an open, honest face and a golden beard and drooping moustache that looked remarkably like those of Sir Francis Drake in the contemporary portraits. Who, I wondered, had dared strike the drum?

"Please," he insisted, "I will push your gentleman," and he leaned over and took the grips in his huge rough hands. I felt as though my bag had been snatched and scuttled forward to prevent his making off with my husband. Philip, seeing me in front of him and realising he was still moving forward, turned round to see who had taken the helm. "I am from Norway," said the fellow, with a broad, kind smile.

There began a wild ride around the docksides. He introduced himself and told us that he was a little bit tipsy, but not dangerously so; he had been drinking with shipmates but had left to find a telephone to ring his mother because it was her birthday. He asked about me and about Philip. At least I think he did. I did my best to reply, and all the while every bit of me was galloping wildly, my legs to keep up with his seven-league progress and my brain to filter his see-saw Scandinavian utterances for hooks on which to hang my random replies. They fluttered in the offshore breeze like ragged prayer-flags. Philip gradually lost his look of shattered apprehension and ventured the odd conversational gambit, though he never relaxed his grip on the armrests. I remembered his casual mention of 'white-knuckle rides' when we were planning our adventure and started to laugh inside, thinking of how I would remind him of the power of wishes and the bizarre ways they have of coming true. I was quite sad when the golden sailor brought us back to where we had started, bowed graciously and left, presumably to rejoin his friends.

I suddenly remembered a similar occasion on our last holiday, in Vannes, where I had often been reduced to tears by his tetchiness before either of us understood that he was ill. An inebriated French sailor had accosted us in the cobbled square and offered me his arm.

Philip had clearly been thinking the same thing. "What is it with you and foreign seamen?" he asked, when his heart had stopped pounding and he could finally speak. I didn't know and I told him so, but I secretly suspected that it had something to do with angels. "Actually, I'm writing a book about it," I said, stifling a grin. "I'm going to call it *Lascar*" "You'll never finish it," he said, and we both laughed.

(*Lascar: cf. Stephen Tennant, brightest of the original Bright Young Things – do look him up!*)

74

Lee-Wah Mets

Another locum registrar. Mr. Khan. We had not met him before but his name suggested several important things about him. Thus I was not surprised to find him dark-skinned and with a pronounced accent. Nor that he addressed himself only to Philip without so much as a glance in my direction. Because I assumed him to have been brought up in the Muslim tradition I did not find this irritating or offensive and sat quietly, without interjection, listening.

Philip had mentioned lack of appetite, nausea and finding it hard to 'think straight'. "This," Mr. Khan assured him, "was often the case with lee-wah mets." Philip glanced at me and I replied with a fleeting blank look. The doctor carried on but my head had gone off in another direction. Lee-wah mets? What on earth could he mean?

Stand-up stereotypes began sliding craftily into my head. *Brummie comics doing pretend Pakistanis. Which comedian was it who used to say he got his wees mixed up with his wubbleyous? Wasn't it Vic Wise? That figures. But that was ages ago and he was pretending to be a Middle-European wasn't he? And there was Sam Weller in Pickwick, but that was a London thing. So it's not racist, is it, to think…? But in this case… Aha! Peter Sellers—the doctor in The Millionairess… Lee-wah. Lee-vah. Liver? Oh, my God, no! … and mets?… Doctors' shorthand: metastases.*

It can only have taken seconds but it felt longer. Mr. Khan was still talking. I framed the question carefully in my head before I let it slip softly into the room. "Excuse me, sir, but are you telling us that there is now a secondary tumour in the liver?" The nurse's imperceptible nod told me I was right. Mr. Khan looked stricken. He addressed us as a couple. "Have you not been informed of this?" Indeed we had not.

Oh, I could understand at the level of principle what had happened. Because he was temporarily suspended from duty, Mr. D had not performed the biopsy. Mr. B had done it instead. We were told that we would receive the results by letter but this had not happened. Mr. B probably thought it was Mr. D's responsibility and Mr. D probably thought Mr. B had done it. Easy. A simple slip-up between secretaries. No conspiracy of silence, no built-in buggeration factor. Nevertheless I felt as though I had somehow been tricked into delivering the death sentence myself.

I had pre-empted the judge's summing-up, but it soon followed. Mr. Khan rang Mr. D's secretary and made an appointment for us to see him in person. We met him in outpatients. He confirmed the presence of a malignant tumour in Philip's liver and swung immediately into a list of extremely positive options, including cryotherapy, chemotherapy and kismet. However, he made no personal offer of further surgery and gave us the names and numbers of the palliative care team into whose bailiwick we would be stepping as we left his consulting room.

We both thanked Mr. D brightly. It was an excellent performance. Had we been judging him publicly, lifting numbers above our heads for the cameras, he would have scored high nines for both expertise and compassion. But the truth lay in the gap between what he said and what he was telling us. It was unexplored territory and we entered it carefully.

Prognosis

It was done quickly. Just a small, clean cut;
it hardly bled at all, and anyway
he had the dressings ready, laid them on
before we got a look at what had happened.

At first we only saw the analgesic
messages written on the clean, white gauze:
Statistics lie. It may not grow at all.
Or not for some considerable time.
There are techniques being developed now...
Surgeons in Cardiff... Surgeons in Birmingham...

When we got home we soaked it in warm water
to ease a growing ache and, one by one,
the dressings floated off. *Buts* drifted loose
and echoed... *given your history...*
due to your age... Assertions came to bits
and lay limp in the bottom of the bowl
as it all sunk in.

I fished out the damp dressings. Useless now,
for none of them would stick back on again.
Only the cold mischief of statistics
had any mileage left in it and so
here we are holding hands across the wound,
feeling it all slipping away, clutching
at randoms, variables and the tails of curves.

The Altered Agenda

Nothing, of course, would be the same again. No amount of telling each other that the deferred death sentence was no different in essence from the announcement 'It's a boy!' could change the implication of the consultant's words. Like those of the midwife, they were an abdication of responsibility. "I've done all I can—now it's up to you."

In another way, though, nothing had changed. We had known when Philip left hospital that the primary tumour had been de-bulked rather than removed and that he had been lent time rather than given it. This made it all the more important that it should not be wasted.

Now we were entering the final phase of the care-package that had been promised to him by the people who collected his National Insurance. We had entered the bailiwick of the Hospice of the Valleys and there began a new set of introductions, notes and appointments. The chief doctor, Richard Lamerton, was an unusual man with powerful charisma. He believed that the last part of life was to be lived rather than progressively died, which, in Philip's case would have involved preaching to the converted. So they talked of other things instead. I think they pleased one another.

One thing puzzled us, though. On the notes that Richard had taken at our first meeting he had written that "Philip lives with his common-law wife, Ann" and since our marriage meant a great deal to both of us we hastened to disabuse him. "I'm so sorry," he said, "but you seem so different from the usual married couple."

It was on the tip of my tongue to ask in what way, but the idea pleased me just as it was and I didn't want to break it.

Letter to my Publisher

14th August 2000

Dear Harry,

Hope all is quiet along the banks of the Tamar.

I am sitting here waiting for the doctor to ring to tell us whether or not Philip is to have another blood transfusion, and if so, when. In accordance with the current climate of political correctness they have sampled his hae/shae-moglobin and weighed it in the balance. Now we wait to see if it has been found wanting.

We have now been passed on to the local hospice folk and we have somewhat mixed feelings about that. On the one hand there is a team of excellent nurses, highly-trained and informative, constantly on call, but these are offset by a rather strange team of specialists who work from a clinic to which we made our first visit last weekend.

Now, I have an almost pathological antipathy to anything that has to be done in a circle, especially when it involves holding hands, and Philip has a healthy scepticism when it comes to crystals and orchestrated group visualisation but, that said, it wasn't an altogether negative experience. The idea is that a selection of alternative therapies are on offer, both to the dying and to their nearest and dearest so I, too, was laid out on a table and massaged by one of the attendant houris. She was slim, blonde, had gold-painted toenails and had recently been swimming with dolphins in Hawaii. I tried to convince her of the similarly spiritual qualities of the palmate newt but she wasn't having any.

I'd never been massaged before. There was a hole in the table and she put a little surgical collar on top and I had to put my face in it while she 'did' my back. Philip pissed off the lady who instructed us in Chi Kung because he really does know more about it than she does and he told me later that he had taken issue with a bells-and-joss-sticks lady who had apparently implied that having cancer was a decision on his part. He asked her where half a century of self-abuse fitted in, bless him. Next time it's acupuncture for Philip— and I simply *must* try reflexology—oh, what larks.

Neither of us went much on the macrobiotic lunch, though (*what am I saying?—we went bucketsful!*) as it gave us wind. It's hard to enjoy being massaged when you're terrified of farting...

Well, Harry—it's half past nine and the street lights have come on and I must resign myself to the conclusion that the good doctor will not ring tonight. Heigh-ho, 'twas ever thus.

Keep safe and be happy

PS. I was hoping to come to the second festival but unless the news is impossibly good or unbearably bad, this doesn't look likely. Good luck.

Doing Without Dolphins

Persuaded here against my better judgement,
feeling the oil-and-crystal ambience,
lying alert and still.

'I swim with dolphins,' says the massage lady,
'it is a mystical experience.'

Prone on the table, through a face-shaped hole
watching my own fists clenching into knots,
thinking—*what if my hands could see my face?*
All jowls and eyebags, slowly dripping down
to form a nightmare physiognomy—
a winner in a gurning competition …

I try to share this with the massage lady:
'Do you know gurning?' 'No,' she says and then
returns deftly to the subject of dolphins.
'They are so good, such spiritual beings;
one knows they know the secrets of the soul
and how to heal it…'

. Her little stroking hands; my tired flesh
shuddering under their ministrations,
my head fighting to bring disparate worlds
to an accommodation.

Spirituality is not my thing
but stretched out at the mercy of a stranger
I did experience a small epiphany.

Some put their faith in dolphins; some cannot.
Somebody who fine-tunes her view of life
by mugging at it through a toilet seat
does not escape responsibility.

I'll seek alternative alternatives,
working on ways of mending what is broken
which do not call for the participation
of dolphins.

The King's Arms

I still have the knife.

We had an appointment with the oncologist, the gentle Doctor Mitra, whom Philip had come to like and trust. Man to man they had talked of how they would handle together the closing months of Philip's life. They discussed chemotherapy and Philip said he would prefer, since the liver tumour was inoperable and his death relatively imminent, to conserve his current feeling of wellbeing at the expense of any possible extension of the time he had left. The doctor agreed that, in the same circumstances, this would be his own decision. Neither of them used the words 'quality' or 'quantity'.

After visits to the hospital we often lunched at the King's Arms. We could park the car a cockstride from the door and so avoid having to use the wheelchair. The landlord had a daughter who made estimable pies; little cups of meaty substance topped with a cloud of puff pastry that responded to direct assault by shattering over the potatoes in oily crumbs. We never met her but we called her Bess and imagined her, like Noyes's heroine, standing to attention over a hot stove, occasionally thrusting a floury fingernail into her long, black hair.

That day we were tackling an excellent example of chicken-and-leek. Philip was pushing his around his plate with a noticeable lack of enthusiasm and I was concentrating on eating mine carefully so as not to make my concern obvious. "You won't want a pudding, will you," he said, suddenly. A statement, not a question. "I want to get back."

I understood; I really did. We had been to see Dr Mitra and found that he had gone. His replacement introduced herself as Dr. Toy. She was small and young and beautiful. What, I wondered, had drawn her into oncology? She was fresh and alive and full of hope. She was friendly and charming, but she was not whom we had expected to see and Philip found it hard to hide his disappointment. She commented on the fact that he had not yet been written up for chemotherapy and said brightly that she would institute it at once. She said she would arrange for it to start on... Her encouraging smile froze when Philip shouted *"No!"* before she had had a chance to pick up her pen. He apologised at once, but without his usual grace. His explanation came out as an uncharacteristic whimper. "Do you think she understood?" he asked as I wheeled him back down the corridor. "Probably," I said. *Probably not,* I thought. *She is too young and too happy.*

And now, in the King's Arms, we were both trying not to look at the shattered bits of the picture we had brought with us, lest we cut ourselves on the sharp edges. Philip was making heavy weather of his laden plate. I paused my penultimate piece of pie halfway to my mouth and said that I would just dash round to Boots to pick up some necessities and join him back in the car park in a couple of...

Philip snarled like an enraged animal — "Oh, you go and do your fucking *shopping*. I'm going home." His chair fell over when he pushed it back and he almost ran from the place, leaving his meal unfinished. I raced after him with my knife still in my hand. We got in the car simultaneously and he drove home in silence.

I still have the knife.

Stage Fright

Living with dying takes a bit of doing.
It's rather like rehearsing for a play;
I'm working on the words, watching the cueing
So as to do the business come the day.
Mine's a supporting role; it's not my show —
I can't direct the action from onstage.
It's hard to pace myself when I don't know
Whether or not we're on the closing page.
I know I'll manage when push comes to shove —
I've never doubted that the final curtain
Ought to be improvised out of our love;
It's getting there that isn't quite so certain.
The question isn't if I can be strong,
It's if I can be this afraid that long.

Nodens, volens nolens

Part of Philip's course at Caerleon was a visit to the Roman remains at Lydney, excavated by Mortimer Wheeler in the Twenties. We signed up for it knowing that it might be difficult but fully expecting to cope.

We had already taken part in a trip to the great Roman camp at Caerleon and even the amphitheatre had been accessible, though the camp itself, chopped up by bumpy little walls, had proved more problematic. Philip remarked that they would have had no place for the disabled in the ranks, but would probably have used them to great comic effect in the arena.

I left him parked in one of the approaches to the ring, sketching the view, and went for a walk by myself. Behind a small clump of bushes I found a rubbish dump and on it one of the metal fingerposts from the sign by the entrance. 'Roman Fortress Baths' it said. 'Baddonŷ'r Caer Rhufeinig'. There was an employee raking up clippings and I asked him about it. "Take it if you want it," he said cheerfully, "it's well and truly knackered. It can't be fixed now. We'd have to make another one. But I'll bet they've lost the mould." He carried on raking.

I looked towards where Philip was sitting. He saw me and waved. Then, with a cartoon grimace, he mimed hurling a javelin at an imaginary lion. I turned back to the man with the rake. "I know what you mean," I said.

Later, when the trip to Lydney was arranged, I helped Philip with background research. The original camp was founded by ancient Britons and taken over by the Romans who mined the local iron-ore. By the fourth century the place had somehow become a trendy Romano-Celtic place of pilgrimage and a fine house, baths and a temple were added to the site.

This temple was dedicated to one of those convenient cross-cultural deities, a two-faced combination of the Roman Mars and the Celtic Nodens. Nodens was primarily associated with healing and we began to see the place as a sort of early Lourdes. So then, of course, we had to go, being as how we needed all the help we could get.

As things turned out, it was a good job we were not being entirely serious.

The Red Mud of Lydney

On a field trip to Gloucestershire, not long before he died,
The tired leaves of autumn were committing suicide
To the threnody of drizzle which was clearly in cahoots
With the red mud of Lydney that was sucking at my boots.

We were following our colleagues to the villa on the hill
With Philip in the wheelchair, doing splendidly until
We heard a noise behind us such as speedy people make
And turned and saw a four-by-four that wished to overtake.

The cure for our predicament was well within his gift;
His flat bed trailer might have offered us a lift,
But he gave the horn an irritated toot as if to say
That he was heading up the hill and we were in the way.

The man in the Land Rover didn't try to pass,
He made me lug the wheelchair through the lateral morass.
He watched me as I struggled but he wouldn't meet my eye,
Just raised his own to heaven with a hissy little sigh.

It took me every ounce of strength to haul it off the track
And I knew as I was doing it I'd never haul it back.
He found a gear and roared away and left us helpless there.
Oh, I would've pulled my forelock if I'd had a hand to spare.

Each time I see the wheelchair standing empty in the shed
Still muddily encrusted in that special shade of red
It galls me and appals and transports me back again
To the loneliness and hopelessness of Lydney in the rain.

Treosulphan

Like an elderly filing clerk that has long since lost the plot, I kept everything. Every identification band, every report that fell into my hands. Including one that was among the papers photocopied from the Hospice notes at the very end of his life. I never showed it to Philip. It was a list made by the palliative care team, a summing-up of his treatment so far, which listed all his many medications. I recognised every one of them, with the exception of *Treosulphan*.

I didn't recognise it. I looked it up. It is a drug used in palliative therapy for advanced ovarian or primary peritoneal cancer, usually administered in courses of five or seven days once a month for up to six months. At first I was happy to believe that it was a mistake by the typist—after all the same document stated that he suffered from 'dry (*sic*) cuspid regurgitation'—but the worry wouldn't go away. Perhaps he really did have it...

But when did he have it? Did they slip it in his food? Was it administered by visiting doctors in hasty hugger-mugger while I was at work?

Or was it something he should have had and hadn't? Was this the chemotherapy that he was told would follow immediately after his surgery? Did somebody suggest it, somebody else assume he'd had it? Philip had been eager to undertake any follow-up medication at the time. He was told that, since there were lymph nodes affected, this would be done. I remember his asking where it would be administered. A doctor told us he'd be going to Velindre, the specialist hospital in Cardiff, and the stoma nurse said it would be done right there in Abergavenny in their special Friday clinic. But in the event it wasn't done at all.

I began to wonder whether he had slipped through the system somehow. I hated games at school. In the fifth form we were allowed to choose between hockey and netball. I told the hockey mistress I had chosen netball and the netball mistress I had chosen hockey and remained undiscovered for two terms, hiding in the library. Perhaps each clinic thought the other was carrying out the treatment. Perhaps those in charge of his case had decided not to go ahead. Perhaps, unbeknown to me, he had refused it after all, even then. But it said on that piece of paper that he had actually received it. And he hadn't. I was sure he hadn't.

Would it have made any difference if he had? And what might that difference have been? What would I gain from knowing the answer? What might I lose by asking the question?

I have visited this thought often, my fingers brushing different patterns on its sandy surface. One day I will go deeper, digging into what I know to be there; all sorts of questions and all kinds of answers, the difference between knowing and understanding. And down at the bottom the insistent stirrings of mother wit and, beyond them, the notion of God.

The Demon Drink

In the late Eighties, Philip had given up alcohol entirely. Since the diagnosis of his terminal condition, he had started to drink the occasional glass of wine and it eventually became a part of our lives; the odd glass outdoors on a sunny day, or the cheap but carefully chosen bottle to accompany a meal.

We saw in the new millennium with Buck's Fizz. A bottle of bubbly that one of his daughters had brought to celebrate our first anniversary, which we diluted with supermarket orange juice. And then, because the fizz ran out before the midnight chime, a drop of cooking sherry.

But, because of old shames he merely hinted at, he never touched spirits. He had bought the Calvados for a friend whose wife refused to sleep with him after he had been drinking it because she said it made him stink of rotten apples. Philip felt that the gift might thus be of enhanced value. It sat on a shelf at the far end of the larder, waiting to be taken on a forthcoming visit to the couple and its unstated subtext made us smile.

Out of the blue, we heard from one of the young managers to whom Philip had acted as mentor during his years at ICI. He asked if he might visit and a date was arranged. He arrived with flowers and a bottle of wine and soon settled into happy conversation. It was a delight to see Philip so animated, juggling memories deftly with this pleasant and personable man.

I withdrew and left them to it but some time later Philip went into the larder, saying that he wanted to offer Rob a drop of Calvados. Moments later I heard him say, "I'm off the spirits nowadays but I'll have one with you." But he didn't stop at one and by the time Rob left he was incoherent and unsteady.

During the night he felt very ill. He told me that I must get him to hospital at once because he had ingested a lethal amount of alcohol. In deference to his terror I telephoned the emergency doctor on duty, who was prepared to opine that the symptoms he was describing were, as I suspected, those of dehydration rather than alcohol poisoning. While awaiting the diagnosis, however, I had heard echoes of what our GP had said about the diseased liver struggling to expand within its capsule and sending ever-increasing waves of pain to communicate its deepening distress. I entertained the thought, God forgive me, that even if this *were* alcohol poisoning, there are worse ways to go.

"Lots of fluids," said the Doctor. There were several cans of lemonade in the larder. I opened them all and left them to go flat. Just the job for rehydration and electrolyte replacement. While the bubbles were subsiding I took him up a pint of tap water which he drank without demur. Then, after a few further swigs of emasculated pop he fell sound asleep and I sat downstairs enjoying the reassurance of his snoring.

I poured the rest of the Calvados into the sink so that I could answer truthfully when he asked, as I knew he would, "Is there a drop left?" The plughole swallowed it a bit at a time as though it didn't like the taste. Then, seconds after the last gollop had gone, it regurgitated a dessertspoonful along with a warm waft of the autumnal wind of it in a farewell belch that lingered in the kitchen like a boozy reproach.

Will it be like this?

Looking to my left, I could see clearly
The curve of your cheek, the light-coloured bulge
Where your shoulder made a shelf for it.

Nearer, your ear, with the unruly fuzz
Of your jowl throwing its perfect outer curve
Into sweet relief against your pillow.

But as I moved to press my morning smile
Into the curve of your neck, I found nothing
But foam and linen, nothing but bedding.

The cheek was sheet, the shoulder naked pillow
Squeezing out of its shrunken envelope,
The ear the swelling round a quilting button.

Panic then, and loss until I found you,
Slid further down, breathing sweet and heavy
In the deep sleep of the late-lying sluggard.

Relief came, and I lay looking for laughter
In the silliness of what had just happened,
But there was only a small, cold question.

Will it be like this when you-know-what happens?
Will I still wake to you when you're not there?
Will I still look for you? Will it be like this?

The Worst Hotel in the West

He said he had a desire to spend time by the sea and I, like the anguished parent of a dying child who dreams of Disneyland, contrived to make it so.

Not that that was a particularly good analogy. No child of mine ever manifested the slightest desire to participate in the *ersatz* aspiration foisted upon a generation by a cynical business enterprise, and Philip wasn't hankering to spend time in Las Vegas or Hollywood. All he wanted was to see the sea.

I needed somewhere not too far away, an affordable taxi ride. I explained my requirements to the Welsh Tourist Board. I said I was wondering about Penarth. They said that if a wheelchair was part of our plans, Penarth would be too hilly and suggested Barry. My first thought was Barry Island and the cheerful plebeian ghastliness that would once have fascinated Philip but would now appal him. I said so. They replied that parts of Barry were quite genteel and suggested a hotel which had, they said, a view over the old harbour where the paddle steamer Waverley docked in summer, taking day-trippers across the Bristol Channel. They sent me a brochure, which repeated all this in print.

So, on the 6th of October 2000, a dull, damp day, we took a taxi to Barry and booked into the Knap Hotel. I had especially asked for a sea view and found we had been allocated a huge 'family room' at the top of the building. I went straight to the window and saw at once why we had been consigned to the upper floor.

All along the street opposite the hotel grew a row of huge conifers, dense and green-black, obscuring all beyond. But over the top and slightly to the left I could make out greyish sand and a boat or two. There would be sea—of a sort—I supposed, when the tide came in. It was freezing so I turned on the radiators and gradually it grew warm enough to support life. Eventually we took off our outdoor clothes.

When at last we felt a quiver of returning equanimity, we put them on again and went out to explore. Philip, in his zip-up fleece, loden coat and flat cap, eased himself gingerly into the freezing wheelchair and we set off in search of the sea.

There was a long flat walk all around the old harbour, with a brave mosaic proclaiming that here the paddle-steamer Waverley regularly picked up its lucky passengers and thrumbled them over to Brixham for a Grand Day Out. Philip read solemnly to the end of the declaration and then began to hum something from Showboat.

"Perhaps steamboats don't need all that much water," I ventured. "After all, the Mississippi is mainly mud."

"Known for it," he replied.

I leaned into the handles of the wheelchair and we pressed on. I remembered him telling me how, when he lived in Whitby, fraught parents would drag truculent children along the winding streets; *we brought you here to enjoy yourself and enjoy yourself you bloody well will...* I took a deep breath and shouted, "Cheer up – you're at the seaside!" but I was glad he couldn't see my face. Back in town we found a warm and happy pub which served good fish and chips.

Later a grubby grey ribbon peeled itself off from the top of the tide and trickled sullenly round the perimeter of the sandy expanse, never approaching the boats. Perhaps someone had tied just such a ribbon around the birthday present, the promising parcel that Philip remembered all his life. He told me once that he had almost died of disappointment when it turned out to be a second-hand copy of Euclid. Can one die of guilt, I wondered.

When we returned to our room, the radiators had been turned off.

At breakfast the following morning the last scales fell from my eyes. It was quite early and we were the only people in the dining room. A girl brought a menu and we chose cereal, orange juice and poached eggs on toast. The girl went to get the eggs and told us to help ourselves to the rest. I went to do so and found that the choice of cereals consisted of a Kellogg's variety pack with the shrink-wrap removed and that there was no orange juice. I pushed open the door to the kitchen and gave a decorous *coo-ee*. I asked about orange juice and was directed to a jug by the cutlery tray that contained weak squash. I asked for the real thing and was told, "We've stopped doing *juice* because the guests used to take too much."

Now I realised that I had inadvertently booked us into one of the archetypal digs that are the raw material of so much seaside stand-up. I thought the comics invented them. I was on the verge of a grin. *Oh, this place will become part of our mythology; we'll dine out on it for years.* Then I remembered that we wouldn't, would we.

Old Boats

There is no water in the old harbour.
The *Sea View* is a snare and a delusion.
A few old boats lie drunken and decayed
Behind the sandbar that denies them life.
Our great adventure ended in disaster
And all you wanted was to see the sea.

I lay down by your side in the stale room
Trying to come to terms with disappointment.
Although I know I teetered into sleep
Weeping for you and me and the old boats,
I dreamed for them the return of the sea
Feeling it for them, happy in the dark.

And, Oh, the touch of it! The merry lick,
The cheeky elbowing of their underneaths
And then the bold shouldering-up of them
From the sucky clutches of the dreary mud.
Now balancing, careful at first, and then
The great tipsy surge of the communal rocking,
Their timbers singing along to the tinkling of halyards
And all yelling together—*thalassa! thalassa!*

Making the Best of it

As Hove to Brighton, as Budleigh Salterton to Exmouth, so Cold Knap stands alongside Barry as a testament to propriety and old standards. The following day we fought our way towards it in the teeth of an icy blast that did its best to persuade us that we should go back. The likes of us, it seemed to insist, had no place among the Quality. As we trundled along I was conscious that Philip's swaddled body in the rickety wheelchair was acting as a figurehead, breasting the elements alone while I, head bent and grimly scurrying, was sheltered in his shadow. "You OK?" I yelled, but the wind flung my words behind me where they rolled backward just ahead of his, which whizzed past my ear, high-pitched and tetchy—"Can't hear a fucking thing."

The weather was truly terrible and I somehow convinced myself that it was all my fault.

Later, we crept out to the Italian restaurant next to the hotel. The fact that it was called 'Porto Vista' added insult to injury, but we felt the need of comfort food. I ordered *spaghetti all'olio*, most basic dish in the world, glumly certain they'd find some way of buggering it up.

I don't remember what Philip ordered. Probably *Pasta Puttanesca*, which had become his favourite since he discovered that it got its name from the Neapolitan whores whose long hours and demanding trade it was supposedly designed to sustain. I looked across at him. With the wreckage and difficulty of his lower body hidden by the table, he had become once more the character I had based on him in my Yorkshire Post columns. He was *Sebastian, my erudite friend*. He held up his hand in mock horror as the waiter headed towards us with a great phallic peppermill and glossed over the poor man's embarrassment by asking if they had a decent Chianti Classico. He was his old self, witty and solicitous, asking me, "How's yours?"

I took my first forkful and felt like crying. It was magnificent. Perfectly cooked pasta glistening with honest oil, draped on the plate with seductive innocence as if it had been dressed especially for this last supper with a subtle dab of garlic behind its immaculate ears.

"Fine," I replied, with a soppy smile.

The following morning I fetched Philip a paper and left him reading it while I went out for a breath of air. The great foreign conifers stood muttering along the pavement, looking self-conscious and out of place, like the Vatican Guard, guarding away for all they were worth but not quite convincing anybody, being too obviously Swiss and in Italy.

I went down the steps into the dry harbour. I had imagined precious time to myself, walking on a living shore, finding things, choosing souvenirs. Here the detritus was not sea-washed treasure, just castaway tat, but I searched among it anyway. It mattered so much that I should find one lovely thing in the forsaken place. Eventually I spotted what I took to be a lost beach ball. Not burst and forlorn but perfectly round and a glorious, defiant yellow. When I reached it I found it to be the cover of a vandalised Belisha beacon, lying where it had been kicked, like the severed head of a hapless aristocrat, memento of some one-off, lager-fuelled revolution that had probably gone unremarked at the time. I slipped it guiltily into one of a million discarded plastic bags and smuggled it back to the hotel.

Philip, fully clothed and cocooned in the counterpane, was asleep. I went to the greedy payphone on the landing and called a taxi to take us home. Then I phoned the Welsh Tourist Board. I drew attention to their brochure and explained that all that stuff about the harbour and the Waverley was bollocks. The lady said that she had had no idea, her source of information being the brochure, which said…

I phoned the Coastguard on duty, who confirmed that a sandbar had formed some time ago across the mouth of the harbour and that the thin trickle that crept in round the edges at the top of the tide was as good as it got nowadays. I told him about the brochure and the Waverley and he said that this was of small significance compared to the current coastal chart, which still listed it as a 'harbour of refuge'. I steered slow astern to our own temporary berth and moored up beside Philip, who was still fast asleep.

Later we sat on the end of the bed, waiting for the taxi. The radiator had withdrawn its services again and we were clinging together like a pair of frozen marmosets. Outside the window the huge trees wuthered and moaned. I started to sing softly, in my best London voice:

> *Wiv a ladder and some glasses*
> *You could see to 'Ackney Marshes…*

Philip got my drift and joined in…

> *If it wasn't for the 'ouses in between.*

All he had wanted was to see the sea.

Tŷ Hafan and the Butterflies

I tried to keep faith with my other life, my persona as a poet—my career, if you will, but as Philip grew weaker I spent less time away from home. My contract at Cardiff had come to an end and I had not renewed it. I still went to Bristol on Wednesdays, but took taxis between trains to minimise my absence. I did few readings now, refusing any that called for an overnight stay, but I had promised to go to a nearby town on the 30th of October as part of a fundraising evening on behalf of Tŷ Hafan, the local children's hospice.

The weather was terrible and the taxi ploughed blindly along flooded roads to the pub. All the artists had managed to get there, each assuming that others might not make it so had made a special effort. There was a capacity audience. The director of Tŷ Hafan, clearly delighted with the turnout and the takings, gave a short speech of thanks and a description of their work with the families of terminally ill children. "We call them our butterflies," she explained. "We know their time with us is limited so we try to give them a perfect summer."

We drove back swiftly through the dull silence left by the departed storm. Here and there policemen were diverting traffic and fire-crews pumping-out and mopping-up. I had the self-satisfied feeling of a good job well done.

Philip's painkillers were no longer holding their own and he had been advised to try Tramadol. I picked it up from the pharmacy and told him I had put it in the burgeoning drug-drawer. While I was out he had begun to experience severe abdominal pain, went to look for his new medication and found the Solpadeine that I occasionally took to ease a bad back. Since it was unfamiliar, he assumed it to be his own new formula, took it as directed on the packet and experienced no relief whatsoever. When I got back he was whimpering with pain and anger and asked what the hell had kept me so long.

I rang the Hospice. Nurse Julie was on duty and came within minutes. She rang the emergency doctor, received permission to prescribe and administer morphine, fetched it and injected it. Philip wept with relief. We both thanked her in faint, frightened voices.

Julie gave me a tiny look that told me she wanted a private word. I went with her to the door. "I know what you're thinking," she said. "But you are wrong and you have to believe that." I must have looked doubtful. "You think that because you have come home to find Philip distressed and in pain, it's your fault for having gone out. But it's not. Our number's been on your corkboard for months. He could have rung me himself hours ago." She gave me a hug and left. Now it was my turn to cry.

The Old Man's Friend

That is a lovely name, almost botanical. It makes me think of a wise apothecary, smiling as he opens his scrip to administer some gentle panacea distilled from rare herbs. Sad eyes and gentle hands. I am ashamed to confess it was the first synonym that came to mind when Julie said 'pneumonia'.

She was calling every day now and the days themselves were short and dark. The streetlamps were on as I walked with her to her car. Philip had been talking about a new weariness he was feeling. His legs were heavy and his face was grey. His chest ached and his breathing rattled. Julie had arranged for antibiotics and now she named the condition quietly and clearly. We looked at one another.

I asked her if she thought he was dying. "I'm not sure," she said, "but I think he may be. How do you feel about that?"

The end had that had been creeping towards us for weeks had now broken into a steady trot. I had begun to see it as a mysterious guerrilla, dodging among a stand of dark trees that hid the horizon, working its way nearer but never quite betraying its position. Now it stepped out into the last of the light and the expression on its face was not triumph but compassion. I thought for a while. "The best way at the right time," I replied.

Julie took my hand for a moment. Then she telephoned Dr. Lamerton.

Going Light

They call it 'going light', the loss of substance
That goes with the failing of the spirit
When the end comes.

My old dog went light just before he died.
His thin bones whispered in his hairy skin
And went to sleep

And all that was left of him was the light
That faded slowly as his eyes went dim;
The other light.

Going light, light going. It was as if
I had perceived a sort of sense in it
For a moment.

Two kinds of light, making an hourglass
Laid on its side between weight and darkness;
The shape of dying.

Death is the snapping of the narrow neck
In between substance and oblivion
And that is all.

And as you come near to the glass isthmus
I wish for the breaking to be gentle.
Go light, my love.

Remember, remember…

The fourth of November 2000 was a Saturday. I woke early and lay beside Philip for a while, listening to his heartbeat until nature called and I crept downstairs for a pee. When I returned, Mavis was sitting on his chest, just below his chin. His breathing was laboured and his face flushed. "You all right, love?" I asked, momentarily alarmed. "This cat's a fucking succubus," he commented, cheerfully. "That phrase has a pleasing assonance," I replied, leaning over to remove Mavis. "No, leave her," he said. "She reminds me of a dog on a crusader's tomb." I changed the subject—"Cup of tea?"

I had rehearsed this day in my head, imagining how it might be, determining how it *would* be. I don't know what on earth had made me think I'd be in control. Just because someone is dying the world does not step aside and remove its hat, waiting for them to pass.

During the morning Selena came to see Philip and asked me if it would be all right for her to stay. She was both a daughter and a doctor but she had come in the former capacity and I was truly grateful for her presence in the house. We had enough doctors, one way and another, and I never asked her for a medical opinion, though her skill was such that I did not need to and I knew that she knew that it could not be long.

After lunch she sat with Philip while I went to take the dogs out and give them some food. As I was running down to Number 8, I passed Phyllis from the next terrace, out exercising her new hip. She started to say something but I speeded up and overtook her, leaving her shuddering in my slipstream, calling out that I was both rude and mean. I turned to apologise, saying I couldn't wait because I was in a real hurry, but she said it was disgraceful of me to run away. Did I not care, she asked, for the children and widows of men who had died for me? Only then did I notice that she was carrying a tray of poppies. I turned again and fled.

As it was a Saturday, Dean-number-twenty-two was not at work. He practised on his keyboard during the afternoon. Its shelf shuddered to the tips of its fixings, which had been drilled deep into the party wall. Over and over again, with true musicianly dedication, he played the same tune, stopping each time he screwed it up and starting again from the beginning. A song popular at the time. The Police. Sting. And try as I might, I could not stop the lyric superimposing itself on the adenoidal *nyang* of the music—*Every breath you take...* The bizarre congruence both appalled and fascinated me.

If I had gone next door and asked, Dean would have stopped at once, but I would have had to explain and the shame of realising, of not having known, would have hurt him deeply. He was a nice man and his music, though occasionally irritating, was never a real nuisance. We could live with it, could die with it if necessary.

It got dark. The streetlights clicked on, shimmered rose-pink for a moment, then grew into their brash amber. "Mickey Mouse," said Philip. I got up and put a piece of MDF over the bottom right-hand pane of the window.

Months ago Philip had cut it to size because the streetlamp immediately outside the window was too bright for him but he couldn't bear to shut out the night sky altogether. It served the purpose perfectly but when I first saw it from outside I remarked that it looked like a broken window. He shrugged and said, "Paint something on it, then. Mickey bloody Mouse, for all I care. I won't be able to see it from in here." So I did.

Doctor Lamerton was due to call at six that evening. I was afraid he might come early and I wanted to speak to him before he came in. Well before six I went to wait for him at the end of the terrace and found his car parked there already.

The interior light was on and he was immersed in a pile of paperwork. When he saw me coming he wound down the window and said he was waiting till six because that's when he was expected and he hadn't wanted to arrive early. I was touched by his thoughtfulness.

"How is he?" he asked.

"I think he's dying," I said.

"Shall I come in?"

"Oh yes—he's expecting you—but..." I realised I was holding his arm. "Please, Richard," I said, "no heroics?"

He knew what I meant and laid his own hand on top of mine for a moment. Then we went into the house together.

Philip greeted him with a smile and extended his hand; Richard took it and asked, "How goes it, old chap?" He had brought a new, no-nonsense laxative to cope with the inevitable constipation consequent upon the new, even stronger painkiller. I looked at the packet, but from across the bed I couldn't make out the name—for a moment I thought it said *Dithyramb* and I wondered whether a *Paean* might have been more appropriate. I seized on the idea with a smile and was busily putting it into the context of a joke to share with Philip when I suddenly knew beyond all doubt that the time for jokes was over.

Because it was a Saturday, many families had opted to hold their firework parties that evening, rather than risk taking liberties with the Sabbath. When the first crackles and flashes began, Philip looked terrified and it didn't take long to understand that he had found himself inexplicably back in London, in the blitz. I held his hand and sang softly.

His face began to change. He lay looking upwards, then raised a shaky hand, pointed and smiled.

"What can you see, love?" asked Selena. "It must be something nice because you look very happy."

In a corner of my mind a Shakespearean parallel caught the light and comforted me.

We had the medical necessities; morphine for the pain and diazepam for the fear. Selena helped me to administer them. Words clicked in the room like worry-beads, helpful and necessary, but their meaning communicated itself more subtly, like the scent of flowers. We sat in silence for a while, listening to Philip's altered breathing and Selena suddenly said that she was going down to get a cup of tea. She did not offer to bring one up, but said, "Give me a call if you want anything." I understood both what she was telling me and what she had decided to do about it. Philip was at the point of death and she was leaving the two of us alone together. May she be forever blessed.

It did not take long. When it was over I went downstairs and told Selena. She went upstairs and confirmed that it was so. "What we need now is whisky," she said. Then she went out in search of fish and chips. We decided not to call out the emergency doctor—after all, there was nothing he could do and there might be a child with meningitis or a road traffic accident. There was nothing to be done that couldn't wait till daylight. Selena went and lay down on Philip's reclining chair; I went back upstairs and found Mavis sitting on his chest, just as she had been that morning.

I went across to the window and raised the blind. On the other side of the valley a few late fireworks ripped into the sky, paused and fell, scattering shimmering gobbets from their smoky tails. *When beggars die there are no comets seen*, I thought to myself. I took down the piece of MDF with the Mickey-Mouse face and invited all the layers of light into the room. They wouldn't wake him now. Then I lay down at his side and slept for several hours, deep and dreamless as the little town of Bethlehem, though the stars were far from silent.

Kevin

The following morning there were phone calls to be made. I rang our GP but because it was Sunday I was redirected to the emergency doctor on duty. I told him that Philip had died during the night and he asked why I hadn't called him out at the time. I had thought it was obvious—to call a busy doctor out merely to peer at a domestic cadaver would have been a frivolous waste of his time. He made it clear, though, that I had got it wrong. I felt guilty.

Then the undertaker. I remembered being told that a local firm was 'good' and their name 'Brown' sounded ordinary and safe. My call was answered by a gentle, strong voice and ended with a promise to 'be with you just after ten'. And, just after ten, a tall, dark stranger entered my life. He came at the worst of times and proceeded to change everything subtly for the better. As he came through the door he extended a hand and took mine firmly. "I'm Kevin," he said, "and until this is over I'm going to be your right arm." And he was.

It occurred to me almost immediately that this brilliant opening gambit was probably a well-rehearsed constant—I bet he said that to all the girls, so to speak. Nevertheless the effect of it, together with his subsequent apparently undivided attention, was a compassionate professionalism that dispelled forever my fears of black crape and unctuousness.

We discussed procedures. I chose among methods, places and containers. Kevin assured me that any of it could be changed without fuss at short notice if I had second thoughts and then said that, if I was ready, he would take Philip to their chapel of rest. He called in his assistant, Dilwyn, and together they went upstairs. They wrapped Philip's body, just as it was, and took it away with them. Not wheeled out on a trolley or balanced clinically as a stiff on a stretcher but cradled in strong arms as though it were the limp and precious remains of a human being.

I sorted out some comfortable clothes for Philip to be laid out in. I chose his favourite Viyella shirt and a fleece pullover Selena had given him. Dilwyn took the clothes to the funeral home and came back later to take me there. Philip was waiting in a simple coffin. The quiet backroom workers in the place had taken the strain from his face and left him looking like himself, asleep. I had taken the mouse-picture from the corkboard and now folded it gently into his hand. In the presence of the dead, little rituals are a powerful comfort. Later his daughters came with rituals of their own.

All the confusing formalities, the registering and swearing and certification, were done with Dilwyn's company and kindly assistance and the arrangements for the cremation came together magically under Kevin's skilled management. He replaced the taken-for-granted cross on the standard Order of Service with a yin/yang symbol he downloaded from the Internet and typeset a last-minute poem with the skill of a serious publisher.

And on the day of the funeral he came to the house and picked me up in the big black hearse. Philip was in the back in his coffin and I sat in front with Kevin. He said this was highly unusual but that I wasn't the sort of widow who would appreciate sitting by herself in the back of a limousine. Which was most perceptive of him.

Press Button. Sit down.

(My script for Philip's funeral—a timed twenty-minute set, performed at Gwent Crematorium on Friday 10th November 2000)

Good afternoon, ladies and gentlemen. We are all here today for the same reason; to say goodbye to someone who was important to us. This is why I have taken it upon myself to lead the proceedings rather than to call upon the services of a celebrant who has not shared with us the thing that links us together—the privilege of having known this one special person. Whether he inhabited your world as Philip, or Phil or Dad, or even as Mr. Gray, he will have enriched it as he did mine.

Most ceremonies in this place will be based upon readings from the Good Book. But to Philip all books were good. I shall quote from some that were important to him.

One of the points that are always made on these occasions is the inevitability of what has just happened to Philip. The universality of the experience, if you like, but it is sad to think that, these days, death is marginalised so that our unfamiliarity with its processes leads to distaste and fear. Philip never felt that. He loved Shakespeare's description of the death of Falstaff so I thought I might read that, but I wanted to ask his advice, as my arbiter of good taste. Then I remembered—he's in Arthur's bosom...

He's in Arthur's bosom if ever a man went to Arthur's bosom. A made a fine end and went away as it had been any christom child. A parted even just between twelve and one, even at the turning o' the tide—for after I saw him fumble with the sheets and play with flowers and smile upon his finger's end, I knew there was but one way. For his nose was as sharp as a pen and a babbled of green fields...

111

It is customary, too, to emphasise that the deceased was special. I think we shall find out gradually, as life goes on, just how special Philip was. We shall miss him most in the places where we expected to find him. Mount Pleasant is going to be different. This is part of a poem by Thomas Hardy but it has Philip's voice in it.

When the present has latched its postern behind my tremulous stay
And the May month flaps its glad green leaves like wings,
Delicate-filmed as new-spun silk, will the neighbours say,
'He was a man who used to notice such things'? ...

If I pass during some nocturnal blackness mothy and warm
When the hedgehog travels furtively over the lawn
One may say, 'he strove that such innocent creatures should come
                                                    to no harm,
But he could do little for them, and now he is gone.'

If, when hearing that I have been stilled at last, they stand at the door,
Watching the full-starred heavens that winter sees,
Will this thought rise on those who will see my face no more,
'He was one who had an eye for such mysteries'? ...

And he was.

Philip lived for seventy years. By education he was a physicist. He played a big part in the glory days of one of Britain's most prestigious companies and later used that expertise in a second career as a wise and trusted consultant. He retired several times but never for long, and he never stopped learning. He signed up for a Master's degree in Celto-Roman archaeology and took delight in his studies till he died. Philip's life just didn't stop till it ended.

He did have a long and uncomfortable illness—but the doctors had predicted a short and messy one. Phrases spring to mind. Positive Attitude. Indomitable Spirit. Sheer Bloodymindedness. All those are summed up in John Bunyan's cheerful poem, printed in the leaflet. I have reminded the organist that the tune is an English country-dance. Will you sing it for him, as John Wesley instructed — lustily and with good courage?

All sing: 'Who Would True Valour See'

Losing Philip is going to be a gradual process. I decided to tackle it as he would have recommended. One step at a time. A Systematic Approach. First thing on Monday morning I telephoned the social worker who was arranging for us to have handrails fitted to our steep little stairs and was hoping to persuade him to a bath hoist. She was out. The girl who took the call asked if she could take a message. I took a deep breath, folded my face carefully and said it aloud to a stranger for the first time. "Please could you ask her to cancel the work at 21 Mount Pleasant? *My husband died on Saturday.*" And she said, "*no problem*". As Philip would have said "Collapse of Stout Party"!

There ought to be perfect words. A poet ought to be able to find them. The words on the front of the leaflet were written a thousand years ago by Gaius Valerius Catullus for his dead brother. Usually translated as 'Hail and Farewell', they are the perfect expression of a liminal moment. But here's where book-learning comes in. Those words were not written for the funeral. He wrote them later, visiting his brother's grave on a business trip to Bithynia.

For each one of us there will come the right time and the right place to celebrate our relationship with Philip, and to let him go. No problem. Or better still, *dim problem*. Catullus wrote in Latin because he was in Rome, so he did what Rome did. Philip was an Englishman abroad and delighted in observing the proprieties. We'll sing him out with *Cwm Rhondda* to celebrate his living and dying in Wales.

So, from both of us—may your life be as relevant as his; may your death be as good. And, failing that, may you live forever!

All sing: 'Cwm Rhondda'

PRESS BUTTON.   SIT DOWN.

Death and the Mattress

It was a good funeral, though I say it myself.

Kevin the undertaker (who knows with what misgivings?) had trusted me to officiate at the ceremony and I had not let him down. I had done my professional best for the man I loved and even the director of the crematorium congratulated me on having managed the thing within the stipulated twenty minutes.

I had planned it with clinical precision, just as woman with more domestic skills would plan a dinner party. Who would be there? I had contacted his daughters, his ex-wives, old friends, colleagues and fellow students... What would they hope to hear? How could I meet their different needs and contrive a memory-gift for every guest to take away? I planted small jokes carefully; each designed to tickle the palate of a few of them at a time. No belly laughs.

Some of the jokes, though, were for us; little nudges to celebrate the shared mythology which had kept us in our fierce *folie à deux* until the end. I wore brown boots, which, according to an old comic song, are a social *faux pas* at funerals. I contrived to use the word 'liminal' to keep a private promise. And I said, for once, exactly what I meant to say. I believe I did him proud.

But afterwards was harder, I had no script for that. I was lost somewhere outside myself watching the ritual file-past; me standing like a vicar in a lych-gate, thanking them all for having attended as they made their discreet getaways, formally touching the widow for luck, as it were. One of his fellow students from Caerleon complimented me quietly on having done for Philip what Berowne, in *Love's Labours Lost*, had deemed impossible — *to move wild laughter in the throat of death* — and I felt the first little crack in the façade.

I was running out of gracious; churlish and resentful were poised to take over. I wanted us back. One of his daughters pointed to her fiancé's sweater with a conspiratorial smile. 'Aran' she said, and I wished I had not confided so much.

Understandably, his daughters had been anxious to know what I intended to do with their father's mortal remains. I felt I owed it to them to tell, so although I had many secret ideas, I outlined one of them. All his life there had been one place where he loved to go, a place he knew well and never shared. He told me once that Arran was where he went 'to lick wounds' because it was the most healing place he knew. I told them I intended to take some of his ashes there and feed them to the first happy breeze.

And now here was this dear, well-meaning young woman singing a descant to my song. A little gob of spite rose in my throat and I was on the verge of telling her patronisingly that Arran, in Scotland, where her father went climbing as a young man, was some considerable distance from Aran, off the west coast of Ireland, where the sweaters originated.

One r; two r's—there was a glorious riposte here and 'arse' came into it somewhere. But even as I was framing it in my head I felt my dead Philip very close. *Leave it, Love. Let it go. We'll laugh about it later, when we're us.* And I could feel the next thought waiting in the wings: *there is no us anymore.* I found one last smile from somewhere and then folded my face carefully and walked to where the undertaker was waiting. He asked me if I wanted to take the single sheaf of flowers home with me. "No thanks, Kevin," I said, "I couldn't bear to watch something else die," and I felt my face starting to collapse like the skin on a cooling rice pudding. I turned to his factotum. "Dilwyn," I said, "take me home?"

At home it felt safer, almost better. I pottered like a naughty child, changing things around to suit myself. I made a space for Mavis to curl up on top of the digibox beside the television. To do this I had to move a videocassette that I didn't immediately recognise; I put it into the VCR and pressed Play. And there was a tall man dressed up like a dentist smoothly extolling the virtues of an overpriced pressure-reducing mattress made of a material that had been developed at NASA for Astronauts. I pressed Stop.

There was a time, you see, when we were toying with the idea of investing in a new bed for Philip's terminal comfort and we sent for all the promotional material, including the bumf for the adjustable bed that is advertised on television by a senior celebrity with a regional accent and improbable hair. She infuriated Philip. I can see him now—every time she appeared on the screen he shouted "Whore!" and pressed the mute button so that she lay on her adjustable bed writhing and mouthing and patting the mattress beside her. It was wholly out of keeping with his image as a gentleman and I loved him for it.

It was he who had sent off for the details of the astronautical mattress. They sent us the video of the blandiloquent salesman and a perfect cube of clammy, queasy foam in a stockinette jacket. "Pity they didn't send two," said Philip. "We could have drawn spots on them and hung them in the car."

It was I who rang the company to ask two questions that were not covered in the accompanying leaflet. What about sex and bedwetting? The customer services representative gave me his personal assurance that the qualities of the mattress positively enhanced the former, but that the latter must be avoided at all costs, since the substance was uncleanable. Bring on the rubber drawsheet? No thanks. Philip and I understood enough about the process to know that at the end the body betrays even the most continent, even the most fastidious. And no part of the man I loved was distasteful to me, even the wretched effluents of his death.

I needed to see the foam cube again; I searched till I found it in a cupboard. I poked it, screwing my finger deep into its insides. Then watched as it healed itself slowly, offhand and unctuous, becoming exactly as it had been before.

By now the tears were flowing, salty and snotty and warm. I picked up the cube of foam and throttled it cruelly. Pity indeed that there were not two, then we could have had dice. Only one, as Philip and I both pedantically insist, is a die. Singular.

I lobbed it across the room in the vague direction of the bin—*Ilea iacta est!* And suddenly I realised that there was nobody left in my life who would laugh at that joke. Oh, Steve, Steve—bless you for quoting Berowne, but you forgot Rosaline's reply: *A jest's prosperity lies in the ear of him that hears it.*

And there's no us anymore.

Discussing Wittgenstein is the compelling sequel to the highly acclaimed *Three-three, two-two, five-six*

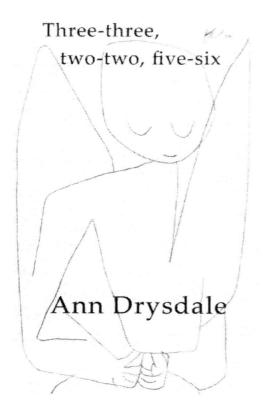

Three-three,
two-two, five-six

Ann Drysdale

A masterpiece, striking a perfect balance between the metaphysical, physical, emotional and institutional aspects of serious illness. What makes it extraordinary is not only the brilliance of the writing but also the profundity of Ann Drysdale's love for this man... the balance between love and fear, distance and closeness, observation and empathy, humour and despair ...something very rare in literature: great art that is also persuasive advocacy on a matter of the most urgent practical concern.

We hope you have enjoyed this Cinnamon Press title.

Look out for Ann Drysdale's latest poetry collection—Quaintness and Other Offences—published by Cinnamon Press later in 2009.

To find out more about our exciting list of fiction, poetry and cross-genre books visit the website at www.cinnamonpress.com where you can also subscribe to our email newsletter and keep up with the latest special offers and Cinnamon Press launches and readings around the country.

You will also find details of our writing competitions and current calls for submissions.

Envoi Poetry Journal

Published since 1957 and with over 150 issues, *Envoi* is a poetry journal with high production values—published as a 96 page, large format, perfect bound matt laminate journal with an eye to presenting the poetry well on the page.

Envoi welcomes all poets, both new and established. Poets from Wales, the UK and the world at large are all welcome to submit to *Envoi*. We publish a small group of poems or a short sequence from each contributor rather than single poems and the style of the magazine is eclectic—we are interested in good poems in a wide range of styles, but with a leaning towards uncluttered, lucid modern poetry, particularly poetry that is willing to take risks.

We also include a substantial section of reviews in the magazine as well as an expanding online reviews section and carry occasional poetry related articles and poetry in translation. In addition, *Envoi* has a tradition of open poetry competitions with cash prizes and winning poems published in the magazine.

A single issue costs £5.50 and an annual subscription costs £15 for three issues. We also have discounts for writing and literature students.

Find out more about *Envoi* at www.envoipoetry.com

Cinnamon Press Writing Awards

Cinnamon Press competitions offer writers excellent publication opportunities. We run each of the competitions with closing dates of June 30th and November 30th annually.

Poetry Collection Award £100

The aim of this award is to provide a platform for new voices in poetry. The winning author has his/her poetry collection published with Cinnamon Press and receives a prize of £100. We also publish an anthology of the best poems submitted and entry includes a copy of the winners' anthology.

Short Story Award: £100

The competition is open to new and published authors. The first prize for a story of up to 4,000 words is £100 & publication. Up to ten runners up stories' are also published in the winners' anthology. Entry includes a copy of the anthology.

Novel/Novella Writing Award £400

The aim of this award is to encourage new authors, enabling debut novelists/novella writers to achieve a first publication in this genre. The winning author has his/her book published by Cinnamon Press and receives a prize of £400. Four runners up receive a full appraisal of their novel or novella.

Full guidelines for all genres:
See www.cinnamonpress.com